THE WIND AFTER TIME

Book One of *The Shadow Warrior*

Chris Bunch

A Del Rey® Book

BALLANTINE BOOKS • NEW YORK

A Del Rey® Book
Published by Ballantine Books

Copyright © 1996 by Christopher Bunch

All rights reserved under International and Pan-American Copyright Conventions. Published in the United States by Ballantine Books, a division of Random House, Inc., New York, and simultaneously in Canada by Random House of Canada Limited, Toronto.

Library of Congress Catalog Card Number: 95-92544

ISBN 0-345-38735-X

Manufactured in the United States of America

First Edition: March 1996

10 9 8 7 6 5 4 3 2 1

*For
Lance LeGault:
a damn fine
Wolfe*

* CHAPTER ONE *

The seventeen-year-old walked into the circle of smooth-raked sand. Around it sharp boulders, reaching toward alien stars, made the circle an arena. All else was silence and the night.

A corpse-white grasping organ appeared, extending toward him. In the center was a Lumina. It glowed.

"Take the stone."

"I am not worthy."

"Take the stone."

"My years are not sufficient."

"Take the stone."

Joshua took the Lumina into his own hand. His fingers brushed the Al'ar's tendrils.

"Have you been instructed?"

"I have."

"Who lit that torch?"

A second Al'ar spoke. **"I did."** Joshua saw Taen standing to one side of the sand circle.

The Guardian forsook the ritual: **"This may be forbidden."**

"No," Taen said, voice certain. **"The codex did not see, so it could not enjoin such a turning."**

"So you said before, when you came to us, and told us of this Way Seeker."

The Guardian stood without speaking, and all Joshua heard was the whisper of the dry Saurian wind. Finally:

"Perhaps we should allow it, then."

Joshua Wolfe came awake. There was no sound but the hum of the ship, no problems indicated by the overhead telltale. He was sweating.

"Record."

"Recording as ordered," the ship said.

"The dream occurred again. Analyze to match previous occurrences."

Ship hum.

"No similarities found. No known stress at present beyond normal when beginning an assignment."

Wolfe slid out of the bunk. He was naked. He walked out of the day cabin, glanced across the instrument banks on the bridge without seeing them, then went down the circular staircase to the deck below. He palmed a wall sensor, and the hatch opened into a small chamber with padded floor and mirrored walls and ceiling.

He went to the middle of the room. He crouched slightly, centering his body.

Breathe . . . breathe . . .

Joshua Wolfe, nearly forty, had used his body hard.

Ropy muscles and occasional scars roadmapped his rangy high-split frame, and his face appeared to have been left in the weather to age. His hair was bleached as if by the sun. He was just over six feet tall and kept his weight at 180 pounds. His flat, arctic blue eyes looked at the world without affection, without fear, without illusion.

He began slow, studied movements, hands reaching, touching, striking, returning, guarding; feet lifting, stepping, kicking. His face showed no stress, effort, or pleasure.

He returned to his base stance abruptly and froze, eyes changing focus from infinity to the mirrors on the wall, on the ceiling. For an instant his reflections blurred. Then the multiple images of Joshua returned.

He sagged, wind roaring through his lungs as if he'd finished a series of wind sprints. He allowed a flash of disappointment to cross his face, then wiped sweat from his forehead with the back of his hand.

He controlled his breathing and went to the fresher. Perhaps now he would be able to sleep.

"Accumulators at near capacity for final jump."
"Time to jump?"
"Ten ship seconds . . . Now."
Blur. Feel of flannel, memory of father laughing as he danced in his arms, bitter—bay, thyme, neither, in the mind. A universe died, and space, time, suns, planets were reborn.
"N-space exited. All navbeacs respond. Plus-minus variation acceptable. Final jump complete. Destination

on-screen. Sensors report negative scan, all bands. Estimated arrival, full drive, five ship hours. Correction?"

"None."

Wolfe's ship, the *Grayle*, darted toward the field on a direct approach.

"Where shall I land?"

A screen lit. The field below was just that—a huge, bare expanse of cracked concrete. There was no tower, no port building, no hangars, no restaurant, no transport center. There were perhaps half a hundred starships, from long-abandoned surplus military craft to nondescript transports to small well-maintained luxury craft parked helter-skelter on the sides of the tarmac. There was no sign of life on the field except, at one end, a grounded maintenance lighter and two men intent on disemboweling the engine spaces of a heavy-lifter.

"Put us down not too far from those ramp rats."

Seconds later, the braking drive flared and the ship grounded. Joshua touched sensors; screens lit and were manipulated as he carefully examined every starship of a certain description. One drew his attention. He opened a secondary screen on that mil-surplus ship, once a medium long-range patrol craft.

"ID?"

"Ship on-screen matches input data on target fiche. Hull registry does not match either numbers from target fiche or the ship listed as carrying those numbers in Lloyds' Registry. Sensors indicate skin temperature shows ship active within last planetary week. Drive tube temperatures confirm first datum. No sensor suggests ship is occupied."

"It wouldn't be. He's already about his business. Maintain alert status, instant lift readiness. I'm going trolling."

"Understood."

Joshua dressed, then went to an innocent wall and pressed a stud. The wall opened. Inside were enough weapons—guns, grenades, knives, explosives—to outfit a small commando landing. The ship itself hid other surprises: two system-range nuclear missiles, four in-atmosphere air-to-air missiles, and a chaingun.

Joshua chose a large Federation-issue blaster and holstered it in a worn military gun belt with three magazine pouches clipped to it. Around his neck he looped a silver chain with a dark metal emblem on it, stylized calligraphy for the symbol *ku*. It also supported, at the back of his neck, a dartlike obsidian throwing knife.

Joshua considered his appearance. Gray insul pants, short boots, dark blue singlet under an expensive-looking but worn light gray jacket that might have been leather but was not, a jacket that obviously held proofed shockpanels. Pistol well used, all too ready.

Someone looking for a job, any job, so long as it wasn't legal. Just another new arrival on Platte. Just another one of the boys. He would fit right in. He stuck a flesh-toned bonemike com over his left clavicle.

"Testing," he said, then subvocalized in Al'ar: *"Is this device singing?"*

"My being says this is so." He *heard* the ship's response through bone induction.

"Open the port."

Joshua's ears crackled as they adjusted to the new

pressure. He walked onto the landing field, and the lock doors hissed shut.

He started whistling loudly when he was still some distance from the mechanics. One of them casually walked to his toolbox, picked up a rag, and began wiping his hands. Joshua noted that the rag was lumpy, about the size of a medium-sized pistol. Platte was that kind of world.

"Help you, friend?"

"Looking for some transport to get around the hike into town."

"Town's a fairly dickey label when there isn't but one hotel, a dozen or so stores, three alkjoints, our shop, an' a restaurant you'd best not trust your taste buds to."

"Sounds like the big city compared to where I'm from."

A smile came and went on the mechanic's lips, and he looked pointedly at the heavy gun hung low on Joshua's hip. "I'd guess you came from there at speed, eh?"

"You'd lose, friend," Joshua said. "When I lifted, there was nobody even vaguely interested in my habits or my comings and goings."

The mechanic took the hint and started toward his lighter. "I can call for Lil. See if she wants to pick up a few credits. But it'll cost."

"Aren't many Samaritans working the Outlaw Worlds these days," Joshua said. "I'll pay."

The mechanic picked up a com and spoke into it. "She's on her way." He returned to the engine bay and turned his wrench back on. The second man appeared not to have noticed Joshua.

After a while Joshua saw a worm of dust crawl toward the field.

Lil was about eighteen, working on forty. Her vehicle was a nearly new light utility lifter that looked as if it'd been sandblasted for a repaint and then the idea had been forgotten. "What're you doin' on Platte?" she asked without preamble after Joshua had introduced himself.

"My travel agent said it was a relaxing place. Good weather."

Lil glanced through the ripped plas dome at the overcast sky that threatened rain but would never deliver. "Right. All Platte needs is water and some good people. That's all Hell needs, too."

The road they traveled above was marked with twelve-foot-high stakes driven into the barren soil. Some time earlier someone had run a scraper down the track, so there were still wheeled or tracked vehicles in use. The vegetation was sparse, gray, and sagging.

"You'll be staying at the hotel?"

"Don't know. Depends."

"It's the only game in town. Old Diggs sets his rates like he knows it."

"So?"

"I run a rooming house. Sorta. Anyway, there's a room. Bed. Fresher. For extra, I'll cook two meals a day."

"Sorta?"

"Biggish place. Started as a gamblin' joint. Damn fool who set it up never figured people got to have somethin' to gamble before they gamble. He walked off

into the desert a year or so ago, and nobody bothered
looking to see how far he got. We moved in."

"We?" Joshua asked.

"Mik ... he's the one that called me. And Phan. He
was the quiet one. Probably didn't even look up from
bustin' knuckles. They're my husbands."

"I'll let you know if I need a place."

Joshua asked Lil to wait and went into the long, low
single-story building without a sign. The lobby was
scattered with a handful of benches, their canvas uphol-
stery peeling. It smelled stale and temporary. There
were planters on either side of the door, but the plants
had mummified a long time before. The checkout station was caged in thick steel bars. The old man behind
it blanked the holoset he was watching a pornie on
and smiled expectantly. Joshua eyed the bars.

"You must have some interesting paydays around
here."

The old man—Diggs, Joshua supposed—let the smile
hang for an instant in token appreciation. "It prevents
creativity from some of our more colorful citizens. You
want a room?"

"I might." Joshua reached into his jacket and slid a
holopic across. Diggs activated it and studied the man
in the projection carefully but said nothing. Joshua took
a single gold disk from another pocket, considered, as
greed strolled innocently across Diggs's face, added its
brother, and dropped the coins on the counter.

"Tell by the sound they ain't snide," Diggs said.
"Damned poor picture. Doesn't look like your friend
was very cheerful at having it taken, either."

"His name is Innokenty Khodyan."

"That wasn't what he used here." The coins vanished. "Another reason I don't have trouble is everybody knows I'm an open book. He checked out two days ago. Took him that long to get a sled and driver sent down from Yoruba. Two other men came with the armored lim. Hell of a rig. Long time since this dump has seen something that plush."

"Yoruba, eh?"

"Three, maybe four hours, full power away. Across the mountains, then northeast up toward the coast. What isn't in or around Yoruba isn't worth buying. The reason they don't fancy a landing field is they like to see their visitors coming. From a ways off."

"I didn't think Ben would change his ways." Joshua nodded thanks. Innokenty Khodyan was running as if he were on rails. "Three other questions, if you will."

"You can ask."

"Is there any other way to get to Yoruba? If a man was in a little more of a hurry."

"You can wait, see if somebody's headed there in a lighter. Somebody generally is, once a month or so. That's about it. Second question?"

"How did Khodyan pay for his room?"

"*That's* something you won't get answered. Try again."

"The two men with the lim? What'd be your call on them?"

"Same sort as you, mister. Except their iron wasn't out in the open. But they had the same kind of . . . call it serious intent."

"Thanks."

Joshua was at the door.

"Now I have a question," Diggs said. "Will somebody be looking for *you* in a couple of days?"

"Not likely," Joshua said. "Not likely at all."

Lil had her blouse off, eyes closed, her feet splayed on the dash. She'd slid the worthless dome back into its housing. Joshua took a moment to admire her. Her breasts were still eighteen, nipples pointed at the invisible sun. She looked clean, and Joshua didn't mind her perfume, even if it made him think he was trapped in a hothouse.

"You stayin' here?" She didn't open her eyes.

"No."

"Do I have a roomer . . . or is it back to the field?"

"Lil," Joshua said, "what shape is this bomb in? I mean its drive. I can tell it's not up for best custom finish."

"It hums. Phan makes sure of that. He says he don't want me to break down out in the middle of nowhere. But I think he just loves turbines. He'd rather wrench than screw."

This time the gold was dropped on the woman's stomach. Five coins, larger than the two he'd given Diggs. Joshua thought about letting his fingers linger but decided not to. Lil lazily opened her eyes.

"Now, that's the sorta thing that *really* makes a girl smile. I *was* gonna rape you for the transport, but not that bad. Or are we talkin' about other possibilities?"

"We are. I need transport to Yoruba. Leaving now. After I get a few things from my ship. That's the retainer."

"Yoruba, huh? You just want me to drop you off . . . or will you be coming back through here?"

"Maybe a day. Maybe longer. I can't say. Maybe I'll need transport when I get there, maybe not. Depends. But if you're available, that might simplify things."

"You just hired yourself a pilot. Ten minutes at my place, then we can flit."

"Just like that?"

"Phan, Mik, me, we don't tie each other down or make rules. They can fiddle their dees while I'm gone, anyway. Build up energy for when I get back."

Joshua went around to the other side of the lifter and over the low hull into the seat beside Lil. She started the primary and let it warm.

"You planning on getting dressed?" Joshua asked. "Or did I just hire my first nude chauffeur?"

"I could put it on, I could take the rest of it off. Whatever you want, since you're paying."

Joshua made no answer. Lil shrugged and pulled the blouse back on. "At least I got your attention."

The track through the mountains had been roughly graded so a gross-laden heavy-lifter wouldn't high-side, but it still was more an exceptionally wide path than a roadway. Joshua asked Lil to take the lifter to max altitude, which gave him a vulture's-eye perspective at about 150 feet constant.

The land was savage, dry brown earth running into gray rock. The scraggly trees and brush were perhaps a little taller than they'd been on the flats, but not much. Lil and Joshua overflew a couple of abandoned, stripped lifters and one thoroughly mangled wreck but saw no other sign of travelers.

There were shacks, but he couldn't tell if they were occupied. Once or twice he saw, higher against a mountain face, scantlings, survival domes, and piled detritus where some miner had tried to convince himself there must be some value to be torn from this waste.

Joshua spotted to one side a sprawling, high-fenced estate. Beyond the walls there was Earth green and the blue of a small lake. There were buildings, big ones, a dozen of them, white in new stone.

"Who belongs to that?"

"Nobody knows," Lil answered. "Somebody rich. Or powerful. Somebody private. He—or she, or it—gets supplies once every couple months. Curiosity don't seem welcome."

She pointed. Joshua had already seen the two gravlighters that had lifted away from one building and now flew parallel to the lifter's pattern. He wasn't close enough to see how many gunnies each lighter held. After they'd passed, the lighters returned to the estate.

"You were in the war?" Lil asked.

"That was a long time ago."

"Figured, by your rig. My dad . . . anyway, the guy Ma said was my father was some kind of soldier, too. Ma kept a holo of him on a dresser, wearing some kind of uniform. Took it with her when she hooked, I guess. I don't remember seeing it . . . afterward." Then: "Any damage in my asking about what happens once we get in range of Yoruba? I mean, I can nap-of-the-earth insert you without anyone noticing. Their sensor techs couldn't hear a fart on a field phone."

"No need," Joshua said. "As far as I know, we can parade right in the front door looking beautiful and getting kissed."

"There's more'n one front door," Lil went on. "You ever been there?"

"No. And my travel agent couldn't seem to find a brochure."

"You better think about cannin' *that* yonk, you get back from your, uh, 'vacation.' 'Kay. There's a whole patch of front doors. Outside the gates there's cribs. Shantytown. Bars. Cafés. Independent-run. If you're looking for sanctuary on the cheap or if whoever you're lookin' for is down on his credits, that'll be where you want to go. Somebody'll be around to collect the tariff sooner or later. Everybody pays at Yoruba."

"I was never much of an alley cat. Except when I had to be. What's the next level?"

"The next stage is straight into the main resort. Up there, what you get depends on what you got."

"That sounds like a good place to start."

"You called it," Lil said. "You want to spend, I'll put you in Ben Greet's lap, if you want. He's the one who owns Yoruba. He says frog, everybody turns green and starts pissin' swamp water."

"Glad to see my friend's doing so well," Joshua said. "Maybe we'll have a chance to talk about the old days."

"I hope you aren't bein' cute and Greet really *is* your friend," Lil warned. "Greet's nothin' but bulletproof."

Joshua smiled.

Something ahead caught his eye. "Well, I shall be damned," he said. "What an utterly *charming* little place."

A nicely paved roadway led up from the main track,

a freshly painted white fence on either side of it and de-marcating the deep green pasture around the sprawling red-brick house. There was a sign on the road below. Lil took binocs from the dash box and handed them across. Joshua focused. The sign read: TRAVELER'S REST.

"Does anyone actually fall for that?"

"They surely do. Pretty regular we hear of some gravlighter that 'just happened' to crash around here. Crash and always burn, real bad, since nobody ever finds the pilot or swamper. Or cargo.

"We call that the gingerbread house. Except you don't have to bring Gretel. The owners'll provide her ... and anything else that's asked for, or so the story goes. Until you stop payin' attention or go to sleep.

"They got themselves a cargo ship back at the field, and every now and then it lifts, but nobody's ever seen a cargo manifest."

"Most places I've been," Joshua said, "after a while people would see to something that wide-open, law or no law."

"Not on Platte, mister. 'Sides, as far as we know, the only people that get done are fools or off-worlders, and none of us took either to raise."

They rode in silence, not uncomfortable, as the track crested the mountain and then wound down across a valley a bit more fertile than the wasteland. There were more buildings, some rich, some poor, no order to their location. A mansion would be next to a hovel, and sometimes there would be a clump of buildings, almost a failed village. Sometimes there would be a paved road, and twice he saw automated ways. The roads, like everything else, started and stopped arbitrarily, as if the builder had built until he got bored or had quit when a completely invisible requirement had been met. There were farmhouses, but each sat in desolation. Occasionally there would be the gleam of a few light manufacturing buildings. Farther on, with no road or track to them, would be a group of buildings that might shift for a marketplace. It was as if an angry child had hurled his elaborate toys across a sandbox.

"I guess," Joshua mused, "when you're studying anarchy hard, logic doesn't come knocking much."

Lil frowned, not understanding, then looked ahead at the track. The frown persisted. She spoke, again without preparation but as if she'd been waiting for him to speak first:

"You know, when I shook my tits at you back there . . . there was a reason."

"I didn't figure it for a sudden impulse," Joshua said.

"I said I had rooms. For a price. Board cost extra, I said. That ain't all that's for sale. Not for everybody, though," she said hastily. "We ain't that poor. And I'm not that desperate."

Joshua maintained his silence.

"If you're gonna be staying on in Yoruba, let me be with you. I won't charge nothin'."

The turbine hiss was loud in the dead air.

"I know, in Yoruba, there's prettier. If you're really a friend of Ben Greet's, most likely they'll be free, too. But I ain't that bad; give me a little time with a mirror. I won't let you get bored. I know some tricks. I was in a house for a while, till I had to offplanet and come here. I ain't just a country dox, not knowin' anything but flat on her back with her legs up."

When Joshua didn't reply, her shoulders slumped. "Didn't figure that'd fly," she said in a monotone. "But Jerusalem on a pony, you don't know what it's like bein' in that hellforsaken port. You know everybody, everybody knows you. You know what they're gonna say, and pretty soon you know what *you're* gonna say ... what you're even gonna think, day in, day out.

"And all the time people pass through, and you know you ain't ever gonna be able to go with them. You're gonna dry and wither, just like this damned planet *grew* you like you were a scatterbush."

"That's not it, Lil," Joshua said. "I've got business in Yoruba, and things might become ... troublesome. Quite loudly troublesome."

"Trouble don't get no cherry off me," she said defiantly; her hand flashed to her boot top, and Joshua saw steel flash.

The small gun vanished. "Hell with it. I don't beg. There's Yoruba, anyway. You want me to sleep in the lifter, or should I find a room somewhere? I'll have to charge for that, you know."

Joshua didn't reply. He blanked her presence as the lifter lowered to the track, which became a paved and marked road with planted greenery to either side. Ahead rose Yoruba, sprawling over half a dozen hilltops, its domes, spires, and cupolas gleaming dully. His eyes half-closed, he let himself flow outward, ahead of the lifter as it moved past a guard shack where a semimobile blaster's muzzle had been tracking them. Two heavily armed guards saluted casually as their eyes noted, filed, categorized.

"Ship, do you still hear this voice and know from where it sings?" Again he spoke in Al'ar.

"You are still heard and watched."

The lifter went up a side road toward a grand series of towers, all glass and multihued stone, surrounded by the exotic plants of half a hundred worlds. They passed through wrought-iron gates and rode over hand-laid flagstones. There were bubbling fountains and, under an archway, two women, smiling as if he were their lover home from his great adventure.

Lil set the lifter down smartly beside the greeters. "Welcome to Yoruba," they chimed.

"Thank you." Joshua got out and knelt, one hand touching the pavement. He *felt* Yoruba, felt the danger tingle, the sparkle of wine and laughter, the shout as markers cascaded, the blank despair of the gambler's loss, the silk of flesh around his loins, the tang of blood and the blankness of death. But not for him. Not yet. He felt no neck prickle. The flurry vanished, and he was touching nothing but a flagstone in a mosaic.

"Is something the matter, sir?" The woman was trying to sound concerned.

Joshua stood. He took a gold coin from his jacket and laid it in the greeter's suddenly present palm. Lil was staring fixedly at the lifter's control panel.

"No. Nothing at all," Joshua said. "It's just been a long trip. Sorry we didn't have time to com ahead. We'll need a suite and a porter. Just one. Neither my partner nor myself has much in the way of luggage."

A slow smile moved across Lil's face, as if her muscles found the change unfamiliar but welcome.

* CHAPTER TWO *

Joshua lay flat on one of the enormous beds, eyes closed, half hearing Lil's gurgles and squeals at their room with its private garden and pond; the autopub with its myriad bottles, flasks, bulbs; the elaborate refreshers with surround showers, deep tubs, saunas; the call panel offering personalized dreams from hairdresser to masseur to escort; and all the rest of the suite's silk and gold Byzantine appointments.

He was reaching out, delicate as an Al'ar tendril, again *feeling*. Again—no threat, no danger.

There was a soft thump beside him, and he was back in the room. "This's the biggest bed I've ever seen," Lil announced. Her smile became sultry. "You suppose it works?"

Joshua's fingers reached of their own volition and ran down the side of her face. Eyes closed, she inhaled sharply and lay back, waiting, lips open.

"Unfortunately," Joshua said, "I was raised pretty strict and never could handle playing during working hours."

Lil said nothing, but her hand came up, touched his, then moved down across her flat stomach, hand circling upward and lifting her blouse. She ran a fingernail over one nipple, and it hardened.

She touched her waistband, and the memory fastener opened. She lifted her hips and slid her pants down until her golden down shone. Her legs parted slightly, and she slipped fingers between them, gently caressing herself. Her eyes opened, and she looked dreamily, smiling, into Joshua's.

Joshua got up. He took a breath, made his voice level. "And you're on the payroll, too, lady."

Lil sat, still smiling. "What do I do?"

"Spend some money. Think rich. You'll need an outfit for dinner. Plus something for tomorrow, casual but expensive. Something you can run in, if we have to. Hair, derm, manicure, massage if you want. Don't get too crazy—I'm not *that* rich. I want you to look like—"

He was looking at an extended middle finger. "I know," Lil said, "what I should look like. Close, anyway. Mistress, wife, or pickup talent?"

"Like somebody who's made a big score would want to help him spend it. The somebody's not dumb, so you're not taking him to the cleaners, but he's got a bad case of lust."

"Who's the somebody? Do I need to know? The guy—woman—you're looking for? Or you? Not that it matters. Like I said, anything you want goes."

"For me," Joshua said softly. "I've never set a honey trap yet. You're camouflage, making it look like I'm just holed up and unwinding."

"Sorry. The men I grew up around wouldn't think

that was an insult. Are you ever gonna tell me why
we're here, or am I just supposed to wait for the bangs
to start?"

Joshua picked up his small carryall and started
toward one of the freshers. "Take two hours. Three if
you have to. I'll be in the bar. Working."

"There you are, sir." The white-jacketed barman set
down a snifter of light amber liquid and a frosted ice-
filled water tumbler. The bar was a long reach of hand-
polished wood and brass, and the shelves behind it
sparkled with the stimulants and depressants of a thousand cultures.

Joshua sipped from the snifter, then nodded accep-
tance, and the bartender smiled as if he really cared.
Joshua wore a black open-necked raw silk shirt and
tight black trousers over half boots. He appeared un-
armed. He still wore the deceiving silver jewel on its
chain around his neck, and the flaring bell sleeves of his
shirt concealed a slender tube projector strapped to the
inside of his right forearm.

The fat man came into the bar from an office, saw
Joshua, and walked toward him. He wore formal wear,
tailored oversize. The man had allowed himself to bald
and was smiling, the smile of someone welcoming a
friend he hadn't seen for a month or so. In the years
Wolfe had known him the pleased expression never had
gone higher than his pink jowls.

"Welcome to Yoruba, Joshua," he said, sitting down,
one careful stool between him and Wolfe.

"Ben." Joshua lifted the snifter in a slight toast but
did not drink. "You look well."

"I always said someone who doesn't respect himself can't have any regard for anyone else." Both of them smiled, flat hard smiles, appreciating the hypocrisy.

"What do you think of my operation?" the fat man asked.

"It's a little flash for my tastes, if you want the truth."

Greet shrugged. The barman put Greet's drink down. It was a single shot of a clear liquid in a spike-bottomed liqueur glass embedded in a small silver bowl of ice. Greet shot the drink back and motioned for another. It did not seem to affect him, and Joshua had never heard of anyone who'd seen the fat man affected by any drink or drug. Greet waited until the barman had replaced the entire setup before replying.

"Garish?" he said. "Perhaps. But my clientele generally doesn't share your conservative tastes. They like seeing what they're paying for up front and gold-plated. Which brings up the question: Who are you hunting?" The smile remained.

Joshua sipped ice water.

"If it's me . . . we might as well start the game now," Greet went on. "And I hope the warrant's worth the risk and you've taken care of your people." His voice tried to force steel. Joshua turned to face the fat man. Something flickered in Greet's eyes.

"No, Ben," Joshua said. "Your sins, far as I know, are still unremembered in anybody's orisons."

Relief jellied Greet's face. "Any of my boys? If so, there's a couple, maybe three, I'd have to give a warning to, even if it wouldn't do them much good. A man has certain moral duties, you know."

"Innokenty Khodyan's his real name. You want a holo?"

"No. I know him. Another one from my old days. He's not using that label, but he's here. Guest, not staff. He wanted secure and had credits, so I booked him into the Vega Suite. You're working a warm track—he only checked in a couple of days ago. But there's just a bit of a problem."

Involuntarily, Greet's head jerked as he saw the ring and little fingers of Joshua's right hand curl back, thumb over, first and middle fingers extended.

"Problem?" Joshua asked gently.

"Nothing . . . nothing that can't be dealt with, I hope," Greet said hurriedly. "You know he's got cover with him? They're contract talent, not working for me, so I can't call them off."

Joshua showed no concern.

"He's fresh from a job," Greet went on. "He's got his stash in a safe in his suite."

"Half a dozen jobs," Joshua corrected. "He went on a spree in the Federation. Hit them high, hit them low. Like he usually operates. But this time he scattered a few bodies around, and people decided enough was enough. So he's mine."

Greet grimaced. "I remember—gracious, it must be ten years ago—I warned him about getting excited. I told him most beings don't get nearly as concerned about property as they do about blood. But I guess it's in his genes or something."

"You still haven't told me about your problem."

"Not with Innokenty. I can't give him to you gift-wrapped; there's some other guests I've got around who think well of him, but I know you don't give a tinker's darn about that. The problem is, he's got a buyer inbound."

"Who?"

"His name's Sutro. He's a pro. I've dealt with him before. You bag Khodyan, I'll have to give him some kind of explanation."

"Tell him what you will," Joshua said indifferently. "You'll have something. You always do. As for the real 'problem,' I assume you're taking a flat five percent off the top."

"Ten," Greet corrected. "And his expenses."

"You'll get fifteen from me. Before I lift."

"Then we *don't* have any problems, do we?"

"Not a one," Joshua said.

Greet's jowls creased as he beamed, relaxed, knocked back his second drink, and raised a finger. "Leong," he ordered. "Two more. And Mister—"

"I'm flying true colors."

"—Mister Wolfe's bill is comped."

Joshua drained his snifter without chasing it. He waited until the barman had arrived with another round and then departed. "Thanks, Ben," he said. "As a favor, I'll try to keep things down to a dull roar and not upset your other guests. One thing. Don't get cute. I'm not fond of surprises."

Once more Greet looked worried. "Joshua, I gave my word. You'll have no problems from me or any of my staff. I'm telling the truth. You believe me, don't you?"

Joshua ringed Greet's wrist lightly with two fingers of his left hand. His eyes half closed, then opened fully. "I believe," he said, "you're telling the truth. For right here and right now. Don't change. Life'll be a lot simpler that way."

"You have my promise." Greet stood, remembered his drink, and poured it down. "I'll be around . . . if you need me for anything."

"One more thing, Ben," Joshua said. "That Armagnac you're pouring's never been within five light-years of Earth. Maybe you want to have a chat with somebody about that."

An hour later Lil made her entrance. Two drinkers at the bar swung and gaped, and one emaciated old man at a nearby table rudely forgot what he was cooing to a bejeweled woman certainly not his granddaughter and followed her passage with enchantment.

Joshua stood as she came to the table he'd moved to. Now he was drinking only ice water.

"Well?" Lil wore solid black, her classically-lined evening gown high-necked, ending just below the knee but slit on either side to midthigh. A single gem at her throat threw colored reflections back at the overhead lights.

Joshua smiled broadly, and the corners of his eyes crinkled. "I am honored," he said formally. "I surely won't have to worry about anyone noticing *me* tonight." He bowed her into a chair and motioned for the barman.

Lil giggled as she slid a little awkwardly into her seat. "I don't have a handle yet on how to do this," she confided. "I don't have anything on under this, and you're the only one who gets the leg show for free."

"Yes, sir?" Leong asked. A professional—his eyes mostly stayed on Joshua.

"Champagne for the lady . . ." Joshua lifted an inquiring eye to Lil, who nodded enthusiastically. "Water for me."

"You're not drinking?" Lil sounded disappointed.

"Maybe some wine. With dinner."

"This outfit really didn't cost that much," Lil said hurriedly. "It was on sale. The man said it was last year's, but I really, really liked it. And the rock's a synth, so—"

"Lil. Shut up and look beautiful," Joshua suggested. "Nobody's asking about the price tag."

The drinks came. Lil drank. "Now what?"

"Now we have dinner," Joshua said.

"You're not going to tell me anything, are you?"

"When you don't know anything, there's nothing to tell," Joshua said.

"I remember," Lil said, "back on—back where I came from, I heard this story. I probably won't tell it right. But it goes something like this: There were these two guys. Apprentice monks or some kind of religious people, anyway. They were bragging on their masters or teachers or preachers or whatever. One said his teacher could walk on water, see in the dark, and all that, a real miracle worker. The other baby monk said the miracle of *his* master was he ate when he was hungry and slept when he was tired.

"It sounds really dumb, telling it, but I never forgot that story. Sometimes I almost think I understand it. Do you?"

"Nope," Joshua said. "Too deep for me. But I surely am hungry. Shall we reserve a table?"

* * *

The fish course had just been served when Innokenty Khodyan came into the dining room. The great chamber, all white linen, bone china, and silver, was about half-filled, and Lil had just been marveling not that there were this many crooks on Platte but that there were this many with money when the three men were escorted to their table by the maitre d'.

Khodyan was a completely nondescript human male. He wore conservative formal dining garb, as did his two bodyguards. One, who had a closely trimmed beard, came in first, eyes sweeping, clearing the room, gun hand near his waistband. Then he let the other two enter. The second gunnie made sure there wasn't anybody in their wake.

"That's him," Lil whispered, eyes never leaving her dinner.

"I'm getting sloppy," Joshua said. "You never should have known it."

"You're not sloppy. I spent too many years bein' the victim not to have feelers out. You lose often enough, you get sensitive. So that's him. What do I do? You want me to shoot somebody? Throw a scene? Or do I just jump under the table?"

Joshua, in spite of himself, grinned, full attention on Lil. "Shoot somebody? Where the hell are you hiding a gun? I thought you weren't wearing anything but that gown you had anodized on."

"Mister, you didn't pay enough to be told *that*," she said mock-primly. "A girl never tells all her secrets. You didn't answer my question."

"You keep eating the tilapia," Joshua said. "But don't distract me for a second."

Khodyan probably was armed. His two men, Joshua thought, letting his *feelings* swirl around the table the three men were being obsequiously seated at, were as good as advertised. They laughed, smiled, joked with the maitre d' and their client, but their attention never focused, always sweeping the room. One of them turned toward him, and Joshua concentrated on whether he thought his k'lmari might be a little overcooked as he cut off another bite. He *felt* the thug reach a verdict— one of us, celebrating, bed partner an import, not one of Greet's doxes, possibly dangerous in the abstract, no sign of interest in us, hence only worth the note—then look elsewhere. Joshua waited a moment, then subvocalized:

"The one we seek is present."

"I am aware. I am appreciating him. My senses are concentrated, and I am remembering completely. Will you be taking action at this time?"

"Not yet. Continue remembering."

He motioned for the waiter as he finished the last bite on his plate, then split the last of the Pantheon Riesling between his and Lil's glasses. "I think we are ready to order our wine for the main course. Could we have the sommelier?"

"You're not going to do anything?" Lil possibly sounded a little disappointed.

"Of course I'm doing something. I'm going to order us some red plonk and then ask about the entrée."

"And afterward?"

"I'm not sure. Maybe some strawberries and port?"

Lil relaxed and managed a smile. "So all you do is

eat when you're hungry and sleep when you're tired, hmm?"

"That's about it."

Innokenty Khodyan seemed intent on a long, thorough spell at the trough. When Joshua and Lil had finished dessert and were leaving, the thief was still ordering, two dishes at each course. "I wish I could eat like that," Joshua observed, not looking back as the maitre d' ushered them out. He stopped at the desk, asked questions, and passed a coin across when he received the answers and a brochure.

Lil remained silent until they'd stepped off the slideway and the door to their suite had clicked shut. She drew a question mark in the air. Joshua's hand brushed the wall. He *felt* no sensors, no watchers other than the passive monitors Ben Greet had installed in all the resort's rooms.

"As you were saying?" Joshua prompted.

"Never mind. I don't need to ask. The wine kinda slowed me down," she said. "I understand you not making your move down there, in front of his goons and all. But you'll go out sometime tonight, right?"

Joshua took her hand and gently drew her to him.

"Cease remembering."

"Understood."

Her lips parted and met his, her eyes closing. His hands held her shoulders, moved down, found the slits in the gown, and cupped her bare buttocks as she pressed against his hardness.

The gown was a pool of black on the floor, and her

hands moved over him, touching fasteners, finding clips, until he, too, was naked. He stripped off the chainknife and the holstered tube projector and tossed them away.

His hand went to the light control.

"No," she said throatily. "I like to see."

He lifted her toward the bed.

It was deep in the night.

"Ah, Christ. Jerusalem. Oh, God."

"Now?"

"No. No." She rolled over, pulling a pillow under her hips. "Now!"

He moved over her.

"Yes. Yes. Now," she said, voice guttural. "Now!"

"Like . . . this?"

"Yes, oh, please, yes. God, yes. There! There! And . . . and the other way now! Do it, God, do it to me!"

Her nails clawed his supporting hands, and she arched against him.

His tongue led him to her nipple. His teeth nipped gently. Her breathing, lowering toward sleep, caught. "Jesus! Don't you *ever* get sleepy?"

"When I'm tired."

Her fingers moved downward.

"You're . . . *not* tired!"

She turned on her side and slid one thigh over his. He rolled onto his back, and she came to her knees above him and guided him into her. She gasped as he lifted, then lowered his thighs.

"What . . . what about *him*?" she managed just before words stopped for them both.

"Tomorrow . . . *is* another day."

Joshua's mind told him it was dawn. He and Lil were lying on the floor, the pillows from both beds piled around them. Lil was sleeping soundly, one hand under her cheek, the other between her thighs.

Joshua went to the window overlooking the garden. He brought both hands up from his waist and extended them outward, breathing deeply, gaze fixed on the space between them. He took the centering stance, then began the slow movements, lifting, blocking, striking, guarding.

When he was finished, he showered and dressed in a casual lounging outfit in a nondescript, friendly shade of brown that he'd bought the previous day. He scribbled a note on a hotel pad and set it beside Lil. The note read: PACK AND GET READY. He opened the door, went out, and slammed the door loudly enough to wake the woman.

"Begin tracking." There seemed to be no reason to speak Al'ar now when he communicated with the ship. He felt the acknowledgment against his breastbone.

He went down the corridor, avoiding the slideway, mind setting aside all things, ship, resort, Lil, the night, the future. All that existed was Innokenty Khodyan.

He carried no weapons.

He asked some casual questions about room service as he sipped a cup of tea in the breakfast room. He studied the brochure he'd gotten from the desk clerk the night before, periodically checking the time. He finished his tea, left a lavish tip in cash, and went toward the lift banks. He stopped at a waste receptacle, tore the brochure into fragments, and threw them away.

He entered a lift that was exclusive to one of the resort's three towers, and touched the sensor for the floor the Vega Suite was on and for the floor above it, as well. The lift went up quickly, floor indicators blurring. It stopped once, and a harried-looking maid got on, pushing a laundry cart heavy with soiled towels. Joshua thought: *warmth . . . sunlight . . . a day off . . . a perfect meal . . . a laugh from a child . . .*

The maid looked at the man in brown, saw nothing worrisome, and smiled impersonally when she got off two floors later. The lift went on to the floor Joshua had first selected.

The resort's architect had understood the needs of those with enemies. The tower was cylindrical, and the ten suites on each floor jutted out independently from the central core, not connected to the floor above or below. From above, the tower would look like a ten-pointed star. Separate corridors led from the lift shaft to the entrance to each suite. In the central area, aimed at the lift, was a sniffer that would be programmed to allow only the weapons a guest, his friends, or the hotel staff carried without shrieking alarm or possibly even opening fire.

Joshua moved swiftly along the corridor toward a suite the desk clerk had said was unoccupied. Halfway down was a niche for a maid to park her room cart without blocking the passageway. He melted into it.

He waited: *wind, wind, blowing, wind unseen, not*

strong, not moving even the grasses, not even whispering . . .

Twice the lift doors opened and hotel employees got out. Neither of them took the corridor leading to the Vega Suite. One glanced down the corridor Joshua was waiting in, then went on. Joshua *heard* the door to the Vega Suite open, a low voice, a man's laugh, the door closing.

Wind, wind . . .

One of the two bodyguards, the one with the beard, moved silently into view, near the lift.

Wind, wind . . .

He checked each corridor but did not go down any of them. He went to a window, looked up, looked down. He returned to his post near the lift door and waited, not moving, showing no sign of boredom or impatience.

A few minutes passed.

The lift door opened and a roomboy pushed out a cart laden with old-fashioned covered platters. The roomboy grinned and said something to the guard, who replied in a neutral tone. The bodyguard made sure no one else had ridden up in the lift, then followed the roomboy toward the Vega Suite.

Wind blowing, embers, flameflicker, fire, fire . . .

The heavyset man inside the suite appeared to be listening politely to Innokenty Khodyan's tirade. The thief's whine had stood him in good stead as a child, and the habit was now unbreakable.

The holoset blared unnoticed, and the ruins of the night's snacks were scattered around the large living room. Doors led off to freshers, bedrooms, a small pool, a bar, other rooms. A hide-a-bed sat against one wall. At night one bodyguard slept there, the bed moved against the door. There was a safe near one couch.

"I'll be peeling wallpaper, I tell you," Khodyan said. "Look. If Sutro don't show today, I'm gonna get a couple of doxes sent up."

"No whores," the bodyguard said. "You told us you'd be wanting them but you weren't allowed. Not until your connection leaves."

"Listen to reason, would you? I was bein' a worrywart, right? When you come off a job, you're like that, afraid everybody's out to do you. I took it a little too far. Right? You guys'll be here. Hell, you can even watch if you want."

"No leg."

"So all I get to do is whack you guys for matches, try to teach you how to bet right, look out the friggin' window at everybody down there relaxing, or else out at that friggin' desert? Shitfire, I can't even open a window and breathe the local air. I guess I oughta be grateful you let me eat."

"Those were your orders."

"Magdalene with a dildo, but you bastards are hard. Look. The essence of gettin' along is knowin' when to go along, right? So how about—"

The door chime went off.

"Breakfast," Khodyan said in relief.

A gun was in the heavyset man's hand. He checked the screen that monitored the outside corridor.

Wind, blow . . .

For an instant the screen fuzzed.

Neither the heavyset man nor his client noticed. The

bodyguard opened the door, and the roomboy pushed the cart inside, the other bodyguard behind him.

Fire roar . . .

A man wearing brown cannoned into the bearded man, driving him into the roomboy, who screeched and sprawled, the meal cart skidding ahead of him.

The heavyset man's pistol lifted as Joshua rolled off the floor inside the man's guard. He snap blocked with his left, and the pistol thunked to the rug. The man had a second to howl, reaching for his paralyzed wrist, as Joshua's open-palmed right hand slipped past the body-guard's neck, index and middle finger brushing skin near the carotid, and the man slumped, boneless. He was dead.

Innokenty Khodyan had his mouth open, but Joshua did not hear what he was shouting.

The bearded man yanked a heavy pistol from a waist holster as he came to his knees. He fired, but Wolfe wasn't there. The blast spiderwebbed a window, and dry desert air rushed in. Before he could fire a second time Joshua was next to him, left hand tweaking the gun bar-rel back, and then Wolfe held the pistol. He continued his spin, dropped into a crouch, and was five feet away from the bodyguard, the man's own pistol leveled. He glanced at Khodyan, who wasn't doing anything dangerous.

The bearded man half raised his hands.

"Good," Joshua approved. "Stay a pro. You blew the contract. Stay alive so you can feel guilty."

The bodyguard squatted, grabbing for an ankle-holstered backup gun. Joshua touched the trigger and blew a fist-sized hole in his chest. The roomboy had stopped squealing and was going for the door, scrabbling up from his hands and knees. Joshua kicked his legs from under him and knuckle rapped, with that seemingly gentle touch, against the back of his head. The roomboy went on his face and began snoring loudly.

Joshua held the gun steady on Khodyan. He back kicked the suite door closed.

"We don't need company," he said. Formally: "I am a duly constituted representative of the Federation. I am serving a properly executed warrant, issued within the Federation and presented to me by a Sector Marshal. According to this warrant—"

Innokenty Khodyan launched himself at Joshua, fingers clawing. Joshua sidestepped, turned, lifted a knee, and sent the smaller man tumbling, almost onto the heavyset bodyguard's corpse. Khodyan saw the man's pistol and had it, fast for a man who'd begun as just a thief.

It was too far, even for a dive, as the blast crashed past Joshua's ribs. He fired, and there were three corpses in the suite.

Joshua walked over to Khodyan's body and looked down. The thief's final expression was petulant. He glanced at his own image in a mirror. It matched the thief's. As a corpse Khodyan was worth only expenses.

Outside the suite he heard dim shouting through the soundproofing; then someone hammered on the door. Joshua paid no attention. He knelt over the body, thinking. Then he looked at the safe.

Joshua tucked the pistol in his pocket, grabbed Khodyan's corpse by the collar, trying to keep from getting bloody, and dragged it to the safe. He looked at both of Khodyan's palms carefully. Deciding that Khodyan was left-handed, he pressed that index finger to the porepattern sensor on the safe's door. It took two tries before the door slid open.

Inside was another gun, which Joshua ignored; a wad of currency from various worlds; a vial of tablets claiming to be aphrodisiac; and two medium-sized jeweler's traveling cases. He took both to a table and started to open one. An unexpected sensation—like small chimes felt, not heard—made him hesitate. He opened the second case. There were three rows of drawers. His fingers went, as if drawn, to a drawer in the case's center, and surprise shattered his hunter's mask.

There was one single stone in the drawer. It was oval and uncut but appeared to be machine-polished. The stone was unimpressive, gray, although there were a few flecks of color, like quartz flakes in granite.

It was a stone the Al'ar called Lumina.

This was the third time he'd seen one.

The last time the stone had been on a headband worn by a Guardian who stood just behind an Al'ar leader-officer on the bridge of a warship, the last of his fleet. The officer had spit contempt and scorn at Joshua and his plea for surrender. The stone had flamed, echoing the defiance. Wolfe hadn't needed to translate to the Federation admiral standing next to him. He turned away from the com screen, refusing to look as weapons officers sent missiles flashing into the Al'ar ship, and there was nothing but swirling fire and black.

The first time had been in a sandy clearing, when a Guardian had given the boy human-named Wolfe his

Al'ar name, the Warrior of Silent Shadows, and told him to become worthy of it.

Wolfe picked up the Lumina.

Quite suddenly the stone flared; the kaleidoscoping colors would have shamed a warmed fire opal.

The fires went out, and Joshua was holding an uninteresting rock. His eyes iced as he regained control. He carefully tucked the Lumina into a pocket. Then, whistling tunelessly, he went to the door.

* CHAPTER THREE *

"I find," Sector Marshal Jagua Achebe dictated, "after a complete survey of the evidence, that the deceased, Innokenty Khodyan, met his death while resisting being served with a correctly drawn warrant for ... for ... you put whatever the charges were in, David, before you final this document for my signature. I further attest that Innokenty Khodyan's body was inspected by me, on this date, and I certify the corpus is in fact that of the charged being.

"I also certify the warrant hunter, one Joshua Wolfe, is well known to me as a reputable citizen who has previously served warrants, on a freelance basis, for the Federation and at no time has behaved in an unprofessional, careless, or bloodthirsty manner.

"This inquest is duly closed." She released the microphone, and it disappeared into the ceiling. Achebe looked down once more, and Innokenty Khodyan's frozen eyes stared back. She slammed the drawer shut.

"That's that. No known estate, no known next-of, nobody gives a rat's ear, so we can crispy the critter after a decent spell. Maybe this afternoon, when we get back from lunch." She went out of the morgue, and Joshua followed her down a long corridor.

"Hell in a whorehouse, Joshua," she said over her shoulder. "When you go and kill somebody, you don't mess around. You could float a lifter through that hole in his chest."

They went into her office. It was big, intended to reflect the dignity of her position, and Achebe had taken advantage of every square inch. It looked like a crime lab had exploded.

The walls were lined with 2D solidos. Achebe looked at one as if she'd never seen it before. There was a line of soldiers in dress uniforms, waiting to be awarded medals by some forgotten dignitary whose back was to the pickup. One soldier was a younger Achebe. Not far from her stood Joshua Wolfe, also at rigid attention. The scar that now etched the corner of his mouth wasn't there.

Achebe tapped the picture. "We were a lot prettier then. At least, *I* was."

Wolfe was looking at another picture. "That one's new."

It showed Achebe wearing a shipsuit with the three stars of a Federation vice admiral on it. She was on the bridge of a ship, staring at the pickup in astonishment.

"Somebody sent it to me about three months ago," Achebe said. "Said she shot it when the word came over the com about the Al'ar. We were off Sauros then, waiting for the landing order.

"She was one of my weapons officers and thought I

might like to have the pic to remember the day. As if I'd forget it, sitting there, trying to handle the idea that maybe I wasn't going to die in the next hour or so.

"Guess nobody'll forget that day, now, will they?"

"Guess not," Joshua said, his voice flat.

"Where were *you* when you heard?"

"About a parsec and a half under you. Waiting to *give* the signal."

"You were *with* them when it happened? On the ground? You never told me that."

"I wasn't with anybody," Joshua said. "I was hiding in a spider hole, staring at my watch."

"So what do you figure happened to them?"

Joshua stared at her, his face blank. After a time Achebe realized he wasn't going to answer her. She slid behind her desk, grace denying bulk.

"Too early for sauce?" she asked, changing the subject.

"The sun's up, isn't it?" Joshua set a skull with a large hole in it on the floor, next to the archaic weapon that might have caused that hole, and eased into a cracked leather chair that didn't match any of the others in the room.

Achebe took two bulbs from a floor unit and handed one to Joshua. He pulled the tab off, waited until the bulb iced, then sipped. Outside, there was the dim hiss of antigrav traffic and every now and then a high, shaking whine as a ship lifted from the nearby field.

"Just to remind you of something you seem to have let slip your mind," Achebe said. "Warrant hunters don't get but their expenses when they bring back the bounty in a meat chest. Even when an upstanding official's willing to say said warrant hunter isn't any more homicidal than anybody else in these parts."

Joshua did not bother answering.

"You losing it, my friend?"

"Looks like," Joshua said ruefully. "I had him cold. I should've hit him with a hypo or a nerve block instead of giving him a chance to make a damned fool out of both of us. Maybe I better start looking for a nice quiet job building bombs or something."

He stared at Achebe as the grin slowly split her face. "All right. What are you holding back?" he asked.

"When you pulled down on Khodyan," the Sector Marshal said, "that put an equally large hole in that 50K Federation warrant you would've gotten, as I've pointed out. However . . ."

She took a microfiche from the desk and flipped it to Joshua. "You need not bother asking for a viewer. Private enterprise triumphs. That's an E-transfer for one *hundred* thousand credits to the being who terminates Innokenty Khodyan's nefarious career. Merry Halloween or whatever holiday you Christians celebrate."

"Who posted it?"

"One Judge Malcolm Penruddock of Mandodari III. Back in civilization. But not that far. It's about—"

"I've seen Mandodari on the charts," Joshua said. "What's his interest?"

"According to the full complaint I used to issue the warrant, he's one of the honest joes Khodyan hit when he was out ripping and tearing. He posted this bounty after you'd already grabbed the official alert and gone snuffling off.

"I guess 'Judge' isn't a courtesy title, because he had

enough clout to com me instead of sending his message through channels. Interesting note, Joshua. I had to remind him the law isn't a private assassination service for rich bastards, since he wanted to offer the reward on the condition Khodyan wasn't to be taken alive. Judges do go and presume they're the only dispensers of justice, don't they?"

"Has he been told yet?"

"As soon as we got the com that you were inbound with a meat crate, I shot one straight off. He authorized immediate payment. So you aren't as poor as you thought."

Joshua scratched his nose, thinking. "Innokenty Khodyan killed some people this time around. Was that what set this Penruddock off?"

"Big negative there. According to his com, he lost a chunk of his gem collection to Khodyan, but there weren't any bodies involved. He was very interested in anything that was recovered. I had him ship me his original theft report."

"Mind if I take a look?"

"You think it's a little strange somebody gets that antsy about a bunch of rocks, too, eh?"

Joshua studied the printout she passed to him, matching it with his mental inventory of the two jewel cases that now sat in Achebe's safe. Penruddock certainly was a man who knew what to buy. Some of the finest stones were on his list, along with their valuation. The two trays of star sapphires Wolfe had paid Ben Greet with weren't there. But the five four-carat marquise-cut diamonds he'd given Lil were. And one other: *small stone, of unknown composition, semipolished, egg-shaped, ap-*

proximately three inches by two inches in diameter.
SENTIMENTAL VALUE ONLY.

The Lumina.

Joshua handed the list back. "I don't know if it's that strange," he said. "I knew a man who collected string. He shot himself after he lost it all in a fire."

Achebe studied him closely, then put the list away and took out two more bulbs. "That's got to be it, Joshua. Just another nut case with money. Surely there's nothing more to it."

Her voice dripped disbelief.

* CHAPTER FOUR *

The slender brown-skinned man blocked the saber slash with his own blade and cut quickly with the long straight dagger in his left hand. Blood lined the upper arm of his heavyset opponent, who stumbled back, mouth gaping in seeming astonishment and fear. Blood oozed from half a dozen other light cuts on the man's bare torso.

Joshua Wolfe grunted, stood, picked up his cloak, and edged his way past the big man's knees.

" 'Samatter, friend? A little blood get to you?"

"I get bored at boat races," Joshua said.

"You think it's rigged? Somebody better check your pupils, bud. I got a dozen large ones saying Yamamoto's just playing with him."

"Yeah," Joshua said. "Yamamoto's at six to five, Lopez eight to one, and who's doing all the bleeding? Plus nobody'll take a bet on anything beyond the sixth, at any odds. Tell me that's not an invitation to dance."

"You just picked the wrong boy," the big man said.

44

"Maybe so," Joshua said indifferently, and forced his way into the aisle. "I make a lot of mistakes like that."

The big man looked after him, worried.

Joshua was at the coliseum's exit when the roar began. Yamamoto's saber and dagger clanged onto the mat, and his arms crossed overhead in surrender. The crowd didn't sound as if it liked what had happened.

Wolfe pulled on his cloak and went out. The streets were wet with the drizzle that had fallen all day. He walked down a block, checking his back now and then in shop windows. He was clean.

He thought about walking back to the hotel but decided not to. He started to subvocalize, then caught himself. His ship was half-gutted in one of Carlton VI's yards for a long-overdue refit and update, so there was no one to talk to. He took a com from his pocket, keyed a number, and spoke softly. Then he leaned against a building, waiting. There was a doorway nearby he could have sheltered in. But he liked the rain.

After a while a red-painted lifter slid down the street and grounded next to him. Joshua clambered in beside the driver. "Sorry to take so long," the driver said. "Everybody's out and about tonight and scared spitless they might melt."

Joshua smiled and gave an address. The lifter went down the avenue, no sound in its cockpit but turbine hum and the occasional buzz as the demisters cleared the windows.

The lifter stopped at the address Joshua had given. Joshua had coins ready and dropped them into the driver's hand. He got out of the lifter and went across the sidewalk quickly, into the café's brightness.

The house musician had a metronome-bass going and was weaving a polyphonic line across it. His eyes were half-closed, as his fingers plucked notes from the squares holoed irregularly in the air in front of him. Joshua thought the piece might have started life as a medieval lieder.

The musician said hello to Joshua as he went past.

A red-faced man wearing a gold woman's wig waved and shouted at Joshua to join them before they got too drunk to see. Joshua smiled, shook his head no, and went to the bar.

He ordered Armagnac and ice water. He sipped, staring at the antique mirror behind the bar, not seeing it. He was thinking about a gray stone and a judge who'd tried to take out a murder contract for a hundred thousand credits. A woman wearing loose silk harem pants and a bare-midriff blouse slipped up beside him. "You don't have to drink alone," she said in a voice that sounded worn-out.

Joshua nodded to the bartender, who busied himself at the mixpanel. "Jean-Claude's out of town?"

"Out of town or with somebody else," the woman said as if it didn't matter very much which. She took the tall glass from the bartender, made a slight toast in Joshua's direction, and sniffed deeply at the gas as it rose from the mouth of the container.

"Thanks for the offer, Elspeth," Joshua said. "But I'm not fit company tonight." The woman shrugged, patted his hand, and went away.

Joshua finished the Armagnac. He dropped a coin on the bar and went back out into the rain.

The streets were as deserted as the sidewalks. An occasional lifter hissed by, sending water swirling up as it passed. Joshua thought he could hear surf crash against the cliffs behind his hotel. A coryphodon honked wet unhappiness from the zoo half a mile away.

The hotel's huge lobby was deserted except for two desk clerks trying not to yawn in each other's faces and a middle-aged man with a short haircut frowning his way through the headlines projected on a portable holoset. There weren't any messages. Joshua considered a nightcap, but the taste in his mind was wrong.

He went to one lift and touched the porepattern lock. The door opened, and he entered. As the door closed, Joshua turned and saw the man with the crew cut looking at him, then away.

The lift had only one sensor. Joshua touched it, and the lift soared toward the hotel's roof. When the door opened, he waited a moment before he went into the wood-paneled corridor. There was no welcoming committee. Staying close to the wall, he walked toward the door at the end. It opened as he reached it, and he went into his home.

The penthouse had a huge multileveled living room, two bedrooms and freshers, a library, and a workout room. Glass doors showed the terrace garden that could serve, and had, as an emergency landing platform. In the master bedroom, hidden in a windowsill compartment, was a steel-wired ladder that could drop two floors to the balcony of a small room he'd leased through a cutout.

Joshua checked the security board. The sensors showed one entry by someone using an approved key and giving the current code. Fires crackled in the living room and bedroom fireplaces. Loughran, the nightman, had followed his instructions.

Joshua closed his eyes, then opened them, looking around as if seeing everything for the first time. It was very neat and looked as if it had been decorated by a man with a lot of money, time to make up his mind, and quiet tastes. It also appeared as if the occupant was a man who'd owned very little for a very long time and who had to keep that little in perfect condition. The penthouse appeared to be just as he had left it at dusk.

Joshua frowned, corrected the slightly skewed hanging of one of the Hogarths, then crossed to a cabinet. He took a medium-aperture blaster and a fume mask out and went to a couch that faced the entrance. He put the mask on a table and sat down with the gun in his lap, thumb resting on the pistol's safety, index finger touching the trigger guard.

Some time passed. A smile touched Joshua's lips, and he swept his hand through the air. His motion opened the penthouse door.

A man stood there. A look of surprise ran across his face, then vanished. He walked into the suite, hands held up to either side, palms facing Joshua. Joshua gestured, and the door closed.

"You're still hard to sneak up on, Joshua."

"You'd better give your boy downstairs some peripheral vision training," Joshua said dryly.

"Hard to find a good op when peace breaks out all over. Harder to keep him in Intelligence after he's trained. Can I sit down?"

"Pour yourself a drink first. Third decanter from the

left's got your brand in it." Joshua put the pistol on the table but left his hand draped over the couch's arm.

The man went to the sideboard, found a glass, and poured a small drink. He did not put ice in the glass. "You want something?"

"I'll get it myself. In a few minutes."

"Aren't we being a little untrusting?" Still moving carefully, hands in view, the man sat across from Joshua. There was nothing special about him. One would never remember his face an hour after meeting him. He would fit seamlessly onto any street on any world and never be noticed. He wore casual clothes in quiet colors. The name he'd given Joshua fifteen years before was Cisco.

"I'm a creature of habit," Joshua said. "Every time you show up out here in the Outlaw Worlds, life's got a tendency to get interesting."

Cisco painted on a brief smile, then took it away. "I've got something special."

Joshua made no response. Cisco tasted his drink. "I understand you blew a warrant recently. Or was that on purpose for some reason my leak didn't know about?"

"You heard right. I slipped. What do you have?"

"I said this one was special, and I meant it," Cisco said. "First I'll give you the terms. Federation Intelligence guarantees all expenses, no questions asked. One hundred K payment on top, even if you draw a blank. You make the recovery intact, we'll pay one million credits. Delivered here on Carlton or anywhere else you want, in any shape you want. It's an NQA—no questions asked."

"You *did* say special, didn't you?"

"I did. And you're the only one being offered the contract."

"I've heard that before, believed you, gone out, and found every amateur headhunter and half of your operatives stumbling around playing grab-ass in a fog they made up themselves."

"You can't blame me for something like that. You know you can't always give an operative all the data before you put him in the field. *You* never did, when you were running someone."

"That was during the war."

"Maybe mine went on a little longer than yours."

"Maybe," Joshua said, tired of the fencing. "Go ahead, Cisco. Let's hear the proposition."

Cisco leaned forward. "There's one Al'ar left alive. He's somewhere in the Outlaw Worlds.

"We want you to take him."

On the terrace outside rain splashed harder. Cisco's eyes glittered.

* CHAPTER FIVE *

Wolfe forced control.

"Hardly a new rumor, Cisco. Surprised that you're spreading it."

"It's not a rumor."

"Look," Joshua said, trying to sound ostentatiously patient. "Since the war, since the Al'ar . . . disappeared, there's been stories floating around that they're still out there. Hiding behind a pink cloud or something, waiting to come back and wreak terrible revenge."

"I know the stories. This one's different, which I'll prove in a second. But let me ask a question," the Federation agent said. "They had to go *somewhere*, right? We were pushing them hard, but it was still their choice, as far as anything I've heard. I've never believed that crap about mass suicide. Doors swing both ways."

"Not this one," Wolfe said.

"Okay," Cisco said in a reasonable tone. "You lived with them. You were their first prisoner to escape. You were our best source for their psychology. So how do you know they're gone for good?"

Wolfe hesitated, then decided to tell the truth. "I *feel* it."

"I'm not laughing. Explain."

Wolfe wondered why he was telling as much as he was; he thought perhaps he had to talk to someone, sometime, and Cisco, at least currently was no more an enemy than anyone else in the Outlaw Worlds.

"*Feel* is beyond emotion, but there's no logic to it; or, rather, it includes logic and uses other senses."

"Al'ar senses?"

"Yes. Or as much of them as I learned."

"Part of why you're so hard to ambush?"

Wolfe shrugged.

Cisco grunted. "I was pretty sure you had some . . . hell, 'powers' isn't the right word. Abilities, maybe. Something that the rest of us don't. Anyway, you've got this 'feeling.' But I can't—Intelligence can't operate on something that vague. We've got to be ready for almost anything.

"Hell, we've probably still got contingency plans tucked away somewhere in case Luna attacks Earthgov." It was about as close as the agent could come to a joke. Joshua allowed himself to smile to acknowledge it.

"Set that aside," Cisco went on. "What put us in motion was the market in Al'ar artifacts. You know there's a ton of people out there collecting anything and everything that's claimed to be Al'ar?"

"Happens after every war," Wolfe said. "The winner

collects stuff from the loser and the other way around. I'm not surprised."

Cisco moved a hand toward his pocket but stopped as Wolfe's hand touched his gun. After a moment Wolfe nodded. Cisco, moving glacially, took out a small egg-shaped stone, gray, with flecks in it.

"This is the current hot item. Asking price starts at a mill—and goes up. It's a—"

"I know what it is," Joshua interrupted.

Cisco handed it to him.

As Joshua touched it, the gem sparkled, sending a dozen colors flickering against the walls. He held it for a moment, then passed it back to Cisco.

"It's a fake."

Cisco blinked in surprise. "You're probably the only one—outside of an Al'ar—who could tell that. It is. Our labs have built about twenty of them. We've been using them for stalking-horses."

"Any luck?"

"None. All we're getting is real collectors, guys who want a Lumina to finish off their collection. If the Al'ar used flags, they'd want one of those, too," Cisco said.

"Why do you give a damn about anyone who wants to buy stuff like this and what's it a cover for? Or what else is somebody getting into that interests the Federation?"

"I don't know," Cisco said. "Those were my orders. Look for anybody after a Lumina."

"So whoever your boss is really looking for must have the same ability I've got—to spot a phony Lumina. Or else you would have nailed someone besides souvenir hounds."

Cisco started. "I hadn't figured that out yet," he confessed. "I forgot ... you were pretty good at systems analysis."

"So you're drawing blanks on one end and looking for this mythical Al'ar on the other, which is where you want me. How am I going to know where to look—if I take the commission?"

"I'll give you everything FI has." Again Cisco's hand slowly moved to his pocket, took out a microfiche, and handed it across. "That's the summary. I'll give you the raw data if you want."

"I do. What did this give you?"

"We've worked various directions. The only one that seemed to give us anything were these Lumina stones. We've found four so far.

"There's a second commonality. All four show up within a given time frame and in a logical order, as if someone was going from world to world and selling these stones or possibly putting them into a network that's already been set up."

"That's a thin supposition," Joshua said. "But say it's valid. Why me? This kind of detail work is what your paper shufflers and door knockers do best."

"Right," Cisco said, his normally flat voice showing sarcasm. "What an excellent idea. To have a whole group of people, who'll sooner or later be identified as Federation Intelligence, wandering around out here bellowing, 'Anybody seen an Al'ar?' What sort of rumors do you think *that* would start?"

"Point conceded," Joshua said. "But still not enough for me to come in."

"Next I want to show you some film. I can't let you

keep it, and I won't even let you put your hands on it for fear I'll walk out with a switch. Where's your projector?"

Joshua rose, went to a wall, and touched a sensor; vid gear emerged. He pressed buttons. "It's ready."

"Before I show you what we've got, let me give you another bit of data. Maybe you don't know it, but we've got all of the Al'ar capital worlds under surveillance, including Sauros, your old stomping grounds. If it wouldn't draw attention, we'd have them under fleet interdiction—assuming we've still got enough ships in commission to mount a blockade."

"I didn't know that."

"The given reason, even to our own agents, is we're trying to prevent looting until the Federation decides what to do with these planets. The Al'ar had some weaponry we still don't understand, even after ten years.

"But that's not the real reason. We put the coverage on because of that damned rumor about the Al'ar being alive.

"Our surveillance is both passive and active pickups. What you're going to see comes from an active bird. Offplanet sensors picked up an inbound ship and decided it was on a low-profile orbit, not wanting to be seen. That aroused some interest.

"By the time the bird launched, the ship was on the ground. One ... person came out as our craft was incoming. Here's the pickup."

Cisco put a disk into the vid slot, and the large screen flashed to life.

The tiny robot Cisco had called a bird flew at low altitude through the streets of an Al'ar city. Wolfe thought he remembered some of the buildings, even though time and weather had already begun to shatter their radiant delicacy. He repressed a shudder.

"Now the bird's coming into the open, into one of the Al'ar parks," Cisco said.

"They weren't parks," Joshua said absently. "Call them . . . reaching-out centers."

"Whatever. Pay attention—the shot only lasts for a few seconds."

The screen showed a medium-sized starship sitting on its landing skids. Wolfe didn't recognize the model but guessed from its design that it was civilian, most likely a high-speed yacht. The port hung open. As the robot soared closer, Wolfe saw movement, and the port closed. The bird had almost halved the distance when the starship's secondary drive activated, and the ship lifted under full power. It roared across the open ground, gaining speed as it went. Wolfe saw the shock wave ripple from its nose, wrecking small buildings as it smashed overhead. The ship pulled into a climb, then appeared to vanish as it smashed toward space.

"Just out-atmosphere, it went into N-space before we could even think about putting any E-tracers on it."

"Somebody has very fast reactions," Joshua said.

"Or some very developed 'feelings,' " Cisco said dryly. "Now, here's the blowup of the air lock area."

Even with the resolution, the picture was still very grainy. It showed the ship's lock, and now Wolfe saw someone moving slowly, as if underwater, up the ramp into the ship.

"Too far," Cisco muttered. "Let me run it back."

The figure backed down the steps, then turned and walked out a few feet into the open ground.

Cisco froze the frame. "Well?"

The being on-screen wore no spacesuit but a plain coverall with a weapons belt. It was very tall and thin, almost to the point of emaciation. Its face looked like a snake's seen from above, eyes vertical slits, nostrils barely visible holes.

Joshua found himself shaking uncontrollably.

Cisco blanked the screen.

"Now," he said, noting Wolfe's reaction, "Now will you go out there and take that Al'ar for us?"

The exercise room was mirrored like the one on Wolfe's ship. The mirrors showed nothing at all.

Outside, dawn was close, and the last of the night's rain clouds scudded overhead.

There was a shimmer in the mirrors, and Joshua reappeared. He held the Lumina in front of him in both hands.

He looked at his multiple image closely. No strain showed on his face.

He stared into the Lumina, and once more his image shimmered, just as he lifted a foot to take a step. There was nothing to be seen for an instant, then he returned to full visibility.

He nodded once, then went to his bedroom to pack.

* CHAPTER SIX *

"Anything to declare?"

Joshua shook his head.

The customs officer put on a smile like a cruising shark, said "Welcome to Mandodari III," and kept a close eye on the detector screen as Wolfe passed through.

Wolfe went to the lifter rank and slid into the backseat of the first craft, putting his black nylon case beside him.

"Where to?"

"Acropolis Hotel," Wolfe said. He'd chosen it from a list the liner's steward had given him. As the lifter rose, he turned, looking back. It was an old habit.

The hotel was as advertised, large, intended for the upper-end business traveler, unlikely to pay much attention to Joshua's comings and goings. It had been built just after the war in anticipation of the peacetime boom that had never come to Mandodari.

Joshua 'freshed, made a vid call, and found he was

expected. He went down to the lobby and outside, ignoring the doorman's inquiry. He hailed another lifter, got in, and gave the address of a restaurant he'd chosen from the hotel's courtesy list. At the restaurant he used their com to call a second lifter and gave that driver the address he wanted.

For a change, the man was no more in the mood to talk than Wolfe was. Joshua concentrated on the city.

Mandodari III wasn't dead, but it was hardly healthy. During the war it had been one of the Federation's biggest fleet ports, close to the Al'ar sectors. It had been hit by raids twice, and Wolfe saw at a distance the shattered hills where something big had gone off.

With the war's end and demobilization, Mandodari III had begun to decay. The streets were potholed and unswept, and the buildings on either side were boarded up or just dark, vacant, their owners not even bothering to pull down the last, despairing LIQUIDATION SALE banners that flapped in the dusty breeze blowing across the city. The people he saw wore the styles of the last year or last decade and were intent on their own business but in no particular hurry to accomplish it.

The lifter went into the hills that ringed the city, past mansions, some empty, some occupied. It grounded outside one, and Wolfe paid the man off.

It was a vastly gardened estate, high-walled with spear points atop the wall, studded with security sensors. Far up a winding cobbled drive was the main house, white-painted with a columned porch, big and square enough to be an institution.

Wolfe touched a com panel and announced himself; he heard a hiss, and the gate opened. As he walked up the drive, he saw movement from the corner of his eye and noted two auto-sweep guns tracking him.

The door opened, and a woman invited him in. "I'm Lady Penruddock," she said. "Mister Wolfe?"

Joshua nodded.

The woman was about ten years younger than Joshua, beautiful in a chilly way. She wore an expensive-looking skirt and off-the-shoulder jacket in gray and a dark red blouse that fastened at the throat. Her low voice suggested that she knew quite well what she wanted and most often got it.

"You don't look like one of my husband's usual visitors," she said.

"Oh? What do they look like?"

"There's an old word. Drummers. It generally meant—"

"I've heard the term."

"They're men who've gotten something that is more than they are, more than what they should have," Lady Penruddock went on, "and want to sell it before they're found out."

Joshua's lips quirked, looking enough like a smile to show acknowledgment.

"I *was* going out," the woman said. "But you might be . . . interesting. I think I'll stay. My name's Ariadne. Wait here. I'll get Malcolm."

Her footsteps tapped away across the marble. The mansion's foyer was huge. One wall was hung with the heads of game animals. Joshua recognized a few of them: an Earth Kodiak bear, an Altairan phract, a Jameson's beast from Nekkar IX. On the other wall was an alcove occupied by a twenty-foot-tall rearing six-legged monster Wolfe had never seen before. He walked closer and admired the taxidermy. He noticed a small square in midair that fluoresced green, barely visible, like a holograph. He touched it.

The creature shrilled rage and slashed at him. The heavy rifle was coming to his shoulder, and he almost stumbled on the green, slimy stones of the planetoid, stepping back . . . and the beast was still once more and Joshua was in the mansion's alcove.

"Clever," he said softly, then frowned and put his hand back on the sensor.

Again the monstrosity came for him, but Joshua paid no attention to it or to the rifle the diorama had given him. Instead, he looked about the canyon he appeared to be in. He looked up at one crag. That was where the shooter, and pickup, had actually been. He smiled, real humor on his face, stepped away once more, and returned to Judge Penruddock's mansion.

The judge was just entering the room, his wife behind him. He was a large, bluff man in his late sixties, white hair carefully coifed, body well tuned. He wore dark, formal clothing, as if to remind everyone of his former profession.

"Mister Wolfe," he said. "I am truly pleased to meet you."

"Judge," Joshua said.

"I see you were 'in' my little device," Penruddock went on. "I've got half a dozen more like it around the house, but that's my favorite. I came around the path, and the bastard was waiting in ambush for *me*. Almost got me before I touched a round off."

"Indeed," Joshua said, and his smile came and went again.

"Ariadne," the judge said, "Mister Wolfe is one of the heroes of the Al'ar War, although not the sort the public heard much about. He's also the man who recovered those jewels that bastard stole from us."

"Ah." Lady Penruddock's gaze was assessing. "I sensed he was something . . . special."

"That's a good way to describe him, and we're honored to have you here, sir. Come to my study. We can talk there."

The three started down a hall.

"I thought you were going out, my dear."

"I was. But I thought I might stay on. Whatever Mister Wolfe's business is, it certainly sounds fascinating."

"I hate to be a spoilsport, but it is fairly private. And I'd rather keep what we're going to discuss sub rosa. Unless you mind?"

Ariadne Penruddock looked at her husband. "No. I don't mind at all. I'll see you later, then, dear. It was nice meeting you, Mister Wolfe." Her voice was nearly a monotone.

Penruddock watched her walk away, then produced a booming laugh. "Women! Aren't they always trying to hang on, even though they ought to know they'll just be bored listening to man talk."

Joshua said nothing, followed the judge.

The den was as he'd anticipated—all dark wood and leather, with maps, guns, and trophies.

"A drink, sir?"

"No, thanks," Joshua said. "Maybe later."

"One of the virtues of retirement," the judge said, "is

being able to do what you like whenever you want. I've found a brandy and milk goes very well before the mid-day meal." He went to a sideboard, poured a drink from a nearly empty crystal decanter with too many facets, added a bare splash of milk from a refrigerated container, and drank about half before lowering the glass.

"I'm delighted, sir," he said, "that you were able to put paid to that vile scoundrel Khodyan. I've learned over the years that there's but one way to deal with men like him, and that's in the manner you did."

"I suppose," Joshua said, "you might feel that way, having been a judge. I've never had that much confidence."

"That's not confidence, Joshua, and I'd like to call you that, if I may. That's just plain common sense." Penruddock emptied the glass and made himself another. "You know, when that Sector Marshal sent me the com of what had happened, I wondered if you were the same Joshua Wolfe friends told me about during the war.

"I did a little checking and found out. Damned pleased to meet you, sir. You did good work, turning all they'd taught you back against those bastard Al'ar. The service you did our Federation was of the greatest, the greatest indeed." Penruddock's voice had gotten louder, as if he were giving an after-dinner oration. "Why didn't you stay on in the service, if I may be so bold?"

"The war was over," Joshua said.

"But the Federation can always use men like you, even in peacetime. A great loss, sir. A great loss. Heaven knows I tried to serve, tried to join up, but you know, my heart . . . well, it just wasn't one of those things that was meant to be.

"But I can tell you, I did my part as best I could. Even though my training was in the civil field, I set up Loyalty Courts and made sure there wasn't the slightest bit of dissent on Mandodari. Men like you, men out there fighting on the frontiers, didn't need to have people backstabbing them with either deeds or words."

Penruddock looked at Joshua for some gratitude and was disappointed when he didn't get it. Joshua walked to one bookshelf.

"Behind this is your jewel collection?"

Penruddock was startled. "Well . . . yes. But . . . how could you tell?"

"Would you open it, please."

Joshua watched carefully as Penruddock fingered a sensor and the false books lifted into the ceiling, revealing a vault. Penruddock touched several spots on the vault's face that appeared unremarkable and then turned the handle, and the counterbalanced door swung open. Inside were rows of shelves. Joshua pulled one shelf out, and gemstones shot up multicolored starlight.

"How many other people know where this is? The police report on the robbery said the thief or thieves—"

"Thieves, sir," Penruddock said. "There had to be more than just one man. They took away half a dozen trays, and I've never known a burglar so bold as to make more than one trip.

"But to answer your question. Myself. My wife. One . . . perhaps two of my servants. Long-time employees, still with me today.

"But all that doesn't matter, does it? You've recovered what you were able to recover, for which I am grateful, and Innokenty Khodyan is dead, which makes things still better." Penruddock looked anxiously at the open door and sighed in relief when Joshua nodded. He closed and relocked the vault.

"Now I must ask the question that's been puzzling me, Joshua," the judge said. "I was told you are a warrant hunter now. Your business with me is over, isn't it?"

"No," Joshua said. "Sometimes I hunt other things than men. I'm interested in the things that weren't on Khodyan when I killed him."

"You mean the diamonds?"

"And one other thing."

Judge Penruddock started and tried to cover it. "Oh . . . you mean that little stone? That was just something of sentimental value. Something I bought when I was a boy, and, well, I guess it was the cornerstone, without intending the pun, of my collection." He had deliberately kept his eyes on Joshua, trying to force belief.

Wolfe stared back until Penruddock looked away. The silence climbed about them.

"Very well," Penruddock said. "I don't know why I'm so secretive about it. It's not illegal to own, after all. It was an Al'ar Lumina stone. How did you guess?"

"I didn't know exactly what it was," Joshua lied. "But that 'sentimental value only' jumped at me. Since no one died in the robbery, there had to be something important for you to post the reward you did."

"You came to the correct end, sir, but you took a wrong turn. I would have wanted the thief hunted down regardless. Have you ever been robbed? It's like . . . like being raped. They came into my house and defiled it. So of course I wanted revenge. Consider this, Joshua. If my wife and I had been here on that night, wouldn't we have most likely been hurt or worse? The police told me this Khodyan had no hesitation about using violence."

"Let's get back to the stone, Your Honor."

"Since you were among the Al'ar, you know what it was used for."

Joshua hesitated, then told the truth. "No. I don't. Not completely. The Lumina gave them focus, like I've heard crystal does a meditator. But it also was an amplifier and allowed greater use of their powers.

"Was that why you had it?"

Penruddock turned around and looked out a window at a huge Japanese rock garden, its effect ruined by size.

"No, or not exactly. I'd heard stories about the Lumina. But I'm not into such metaphysical—" Penruddock hesitated before going on, "—stuff. I wanted it as a trophy. Most of my gems have a history, and I know their value, not just in money. Some have been the ruin of a family or a dynasty, some have been part of a reluctant bride's price, and so forth. This Lumina was the price of empire for us."

Joshua knew Penruddock was lying.

"What do you think happened to it?" the judge went on.

"I don't know. Innokenty Khodyan hadn't linked up with his fence when I took him, and supposedly nobody else on Platte had gotten any jewels from him."

"Then he must have sold it before he reached whatever godforsaken world you killed him on. Certainly there's no market for it on Mandodari III."

"Possibly," Joshua said. "Or else he had already made the delivery to his customer."

"What do you mean?"

"Innokenty Khodyan was a professional. Some of the dozen thefts he pulled before I took him were general—he'd found out about someone's stash and gone after it.

"But this would appear to be something different. I'd suspect the theft was commissioned."

"For the Lumina?" Penruddock looked shaken.

"There are other collectors of Al'ar gear," Joshua pressed. "Do you know any of them? Better, have any of them come here and seen the Lumina?"

"No to both of your questions," Penruddock said flatly. "I've heard about those wretches, with their bits of uniforms and parts of shot-down ships . . . thank you, I am hardly of their ilk."

"Where did you get the Lumina?"

"I can't tell you."

"Was it here on Mandodari?" Joshua caught and held Penruddock's gaze.

"I said I can't—"

"You just did. Who sold it to you?"

"A man contacted me directly," Penruddock said grudgingly.

"How did he know you were interested?"

"I'd mentioned what I wanted to some friends."

"Other gem collectors?"

"Yes. One had told me he'd heard of a Lumina—actually that there were two, for sale, but they were far beyond his price."

"Where is he now?"

"He's dead. He died . . . natural causes . . . about two months after I bought the stone."

"The man you bought it from here. Was he a native of Mandodari?"

"No. I met him at the spaceport. He said he was between ships."

"Do you know where he came from? Where he was going?"

"No. I only cared about what he wanted to sell."

"How'd you pay?"

"Cash."

"How much?"

Penruddock looked stubborn.

"How much?"

"Two million five hundred," he said.

"That's a great deal of money for something you're just going to leave in a vault and just look at once a week or so. What else did you plan to do with it?"

"I already said—nothing. It was merely to *have* it! You're not a collector, so you wouldn't understand."

"Maybe I wouldn't," Wolfe said. "Have you ever heard of a man named Sutro?"

"Never."

Joshua searched for his next question.

"I didn't expect this when I allowed you to come here," Penruddock said. "To be grilled like I was some kind of criminal."

"So the Lumina's gone, and you have no idea who might have taken it," Wolfe went on, paying no mind to the judge's words. "Do you want it back?"

"Yes . . . no."

"Make up your mind."

"I don't want that stone back. I don't think you could recover it," Penruddock said. "Especially if what you said is true and another collector sent that son of a bitch Khodyan to steal it from me. But I want another one."

"That doesn't make sense."

"I don't have to make sense, Wolfe," the judge said, trying to regain control of the situation. "Perhaps I just realized it myself. You said you came here looking for warrant work. Very well. You've got it. I'll cover your expenses and pay you a finder's fee when you secure me a second Lumina. I'll pay the same price as I did for the first."

Joshua walked across the room and stared down at the mansion's front entrance and driveway. He heard a slight noise, and a small metallic green lifter came into view, hovering down the drive and out the gate. Joshua turned back.

"If I take the warrant," he said, "I'll want the rest of what you're not telling me."

"What are you saying?"

"I'll need to know who the man was you bought it from, how he got in contact with you, where he came from, and why you trusted him enough to go to a spaceport with that much cold cash. Just for a beginning."

"I told you everything!"

Joshua Wolfe took one of the hotel's cards from a pocket and laid it on a table.

"You can reach me here."

The gate closed behind Joshua, and he started back toward the city. He heard a turbine whine, turned, and saw the metallic green lifter. Ariadne Penruddock was at the controls. She stopped the craft, and the window hissed down.

"It's a long walk, even if it's downhill. Need a ride?"

"I never walk unless I have to."

Joshua went around the back of the vehicle and opened the door. He looked back up the drive at the house. In an upper-story window he saw a white blur that might have been a face.

He got in and slid the door closed.

"I'm at the Acropolis," he said.

"Mister Wolfe, would you mind if we had a talk?"

"Not at all. What about?"

"My husband. Lumina stones."

"I *felt* someone else's presence while we were talking," Joshua said. "Were you eavesdropping . . . or are you more sophisticated?"

Without taking her eyes from the road, Lady Penruddock opened her purse and showed him a small com. "Sometimes a woman needs to know what's being said about her even if she's away from the house. I had the pickup put in his study just after we were married."

"Maybe," Wolfe suggested, "you'd better pick a place for our talk where you're not known."

"The Acropolis is fine. Nobody in our circle goes there."

The bar was automated, which meant one less witness. It was empty except for two salesmen nursing beers and glowering at their notebook screens as if they were the supervisors who'd given them this awful territory. Ariadne studied the menu set into the tabletop.

"Deneb sherry," she decided, and touched the correct sensor.

There were no Armagnacs, but there was a local pomace brandy. The delivery slot opened, and Lady Penruddock's drink and Wolfe's water and brandy appeared. He fingered the tab sensor, touched the snifter to his lips and drank ice water.

"Let me tell you about my husband and myself," Ariadne said without preamble. "We married for our own separate reasons, and for me at least, nothing has altered my intent.

"Malcolm and I largely lead our own lives. What he does is his business. If he wishes me to accompany him, I am delighted. If not . . ." She shrugged. "I have my own friends, my own pursuits. Malcolm cares little what I do so long as I do not embarrass him or force him to take notice.

"If I found you attractive, which I do, and we happened to spend some time together, that would only concern the two of us.

"I am not sure, though, that that would be wise. For me. But I am still thinking about it." Her fingers touched the fastener of her blouse for an instant, then went away.

"What Malcolm perhaps does not yet realize is that I require the same from him. He must not embarrass me or force me to have to apologize for his sometimes unusual predilections."

"Such as the Lumina?"

"Exactly. Did you know he was lying when he said he only wished to own the Lumina for itself?"

"I did."

"My husband is a devotee of power," Ariadne said carefully. "He chose to become a civil judge for that reason, instead of criminal law. That was well before the war, when our world was thriving.

"Malcolm made his decisions wisely over the years, not so much for justice as for how they might benefit him. He was quite successful.

"Then the war ruined him, as it ruined this world. When it was over and the Federation left, all the wonderful wheelings and dealings with land, and estates, and investments, on- and offworld, were mostly gone.

"Malcolm had planned to use his Loyalty Courts to propel him into politics, possibly to the highest offices. But with peace came the new government, which holds office by the size of the welfare checks it gives out."

She shrugged. "I care nothing about that or about what the working man does or thinks.

"Malcolm retired from the bench at the advice of several lawyers who said there might otherwise be an investigation of his decisions before and during the war.

"So he looked about for other fields to conquer.

"One of them was me. My family had been very indiscreet in war investments, so our standing with the hoi polloi was shaky. Also, I'd been a bit . . . indiscreet once when I was very, very young. Mandodari doesn't care what goes on in its bedrooms so long as the windows are blanked. I wasn't that cautious. The woman and her husband were able to leave, but I was trapped here, and Malcolm was a most convenient salvation.

"You look surprised, Mister Wolfe. Isn't a woman permitted to be honest about herself and her chances?"

"I'm just surprised you're telling all this to a stranger."

"Why not? Better to a stranger, one that'll be off-world in a few days, than to the whale-mouthed gossips I normally associate with. As I was saying, marriage benefited us both. Malcolm received certain material advantages, perhaps what was known as a dowry in the old days, and I became a quote honest end quote woman.

"After we were married, Malcolm started hearing about the Lumina stone. He already had his collection of jewels, which I truthfully believe is the only thing he completely loves, and so it didn't seem that odd for him to want an Al'ar stone."

"The Lumina is not a jewel."

"And how many people know that? Let me continue. He felt that possession of a Lumina stone could bring him some feeling for power that might guide him to his next step.

"At least that was what he thought when he began his quest. Then he heard about the *ur*-Lumina."

"The *what*?"

"Now it's my turn for surprise. I thought you would have known of that, since I heard Malcolm say you were among the Al'ar, although I'm not sure I completely understand.

"Malcolm heard stories of a great Lumina, although I don't know if anyone ever said anything about its physical size. I've heard him call it a 'king Lumina' or a 'mother Lumina.' He didn't tell me what it was used for, what it was meant to do. But if a small Lumina had the purpose you told Malcolm, the great one would surely be worth possessing.

"He was going to use the Lumina he had to track down the big one. I don't know how. Maybe he thought it would lead him directly; maybe he thought whoever he bought the stone from could help him. He was never that specific. Now he wants to hire you for the search."

Joshua rolled brandy around his mouth, concentrating on the burn, letting the words find their own meaning. He took a second swallow.

"Very well," he said. "You were honest with me, and I'll return the trade. I've never heard of this ultimate Lumina, not even when I was a boy and was among them. I don't see how such a thing could even exist. If it did, it would have been at least hinted at in their ceremonies."

"You could be right," Ariadne said indifferently. She touched the menu for another sherry. "It doesn't really matter to me."

"All right," Joshua said. "So what do *you* want me to do about your husband?"

"You can take the commission if you wish," Lady Penruddock said. "All I ask is you keep Malcolm from making an utter fool of himself—or getting hurt.

"I can guess you have your own agenda with this Lumina stone and don't know what it is or care.

"All I'm concerned about is Malcolm. Do what I want, and I'll be a friend. A very good friend. Otherwise ... well, my family may be in disgrace, but we still have enough power to make life exceedingly miserable for you even if you are some kind of war hero, even out into the Outlaw Worlds."

She drank most of her drink. "As for that other thing I spoke of, whatever might happen between you and me . . . that can wait until another time."

She dipped a finger into the dregs of the sherry, touched it to Joshua's lips, got up, and walked out of the bar, not looking back.

Joshua sat very still for a time. He picked up his snifter, was about to drink, then put the glass down, signed the tab with a fingerprint, and went out of the hotel into the dusk.

* CHAPTER SEVEN *

"Twenny-five credits for straight, thirty-five for a suckoff, fifty for roun' th' worl', an' for a hunnerd you can have me *an'* Irina," the woman said, trying to sound as if it mattered which was chosen. Her partner smiled in Wolfe's general vicinity, then turned as a lifter approached and saluted it with her chest. She looked disappointed when the driver didn't slow down.

"Suppose I'm interested in something else," Joshua said.

"Like what? I don't do pain or shit ... but I can send you to somebody who does." The woman leaned back against the wall of the bar. "Shoulda known you weren't th' kind who wants somethin' normal. Guys who look like you never do."

"Not that, either," Wolfe said. "I think you might be needing a new fancy man."

"Not a chance. Keos takes real good care a me an' Irina an' the other girls."

"I didn't say I was asking."

76

"Get on your scooter, bud. Or you're gonna get hurt."

Joshua didn't move. The woman's hand dove in her purse and came out with a silent alarm. "You're lookin' for trouble, you're 'bout to get on kissin' terms with it."

The other woman came closer, her eyes wide. She licked her lips in anticipation.

A man came out of the bar, hand inside his vest. He was big and walked with a limp, and the surgeon who'd rebuilt the side of his face hadn't done a very good job.

"What is it, Marla?"

"Him," the first woman said. "He wants t' be our new mack."

"Shit!" the man spit, and came in on Joshua, hand coming out of the vest with a sap. Joshua stepped into him, and two fingers rapped sharply on the man's forehead as Wolfe struck the pimp's forearm with the side of his blocking hand.

The blackjack hit the filthy pavement before the man did.

The two whores looked scared. Joshua kept one eye on them while he knelt and rifled through the man's pockets. He found a knife, a wad of cash, a vial containing a brownish powder, and a flat blaster in an ankle holster. He threw the vial and knife into the street and tossed the credits to Marla.

"Thanks," he said, slipping the blaster into his pocket, and started away.

Marla stared after him, completely bewildered. "Hey! I thought you was—"

But Wolfe was around the corner and gone with what he'd gone into the port district for.

* * *

The message light on his com was blinking when he got back to the hotel.

"Mister Wolfe?" It was Penruddock's voice. "I've been considering what you said earlier. Perhaps it would be convenient for you to come back out here, and we can continue our discussion. We'll be in all evening."

Joshua carefully checked the gun he'd acquired before returning the call.

"This'll be fine," he told the lifter driver, and gave him credits. He got out and started for the eight-sided, five-story blue monstrosity the band's efforts blared from.

The lifter took off, and Joshua turned in his tracks and went down three streets and over two until he was on the street where the Penruddocks lived.

He buzzed the gate panel and was admitted.

Panels sensed his approach and lit, and the driveway was a long, cobbled finger of soft light through the night.

The Penruddocks met him at the door. Malcolm wore a soft red dressing gown over black dress pants and an open-necked shirt. Ariadne Penruddock wore a green silk robe that would have been modest except for the long slit that ran up the left side to her hip. She caught Wolfe's glance and moved her leg slightly, and Joshua saw tanned smoothness ending in close-cropped darkness. Both Wolfe and Penruddock pretended not to notice what she'd done.

"I'm glad we're going to have a chance—" Penruddock broke off at the scream of the engines.

Two gravlighters came in above the tree line. Wolfe saw the gunmen on the open deck and dove into Penruddock.

Ariadne's mouth gaped with surprise. Wolfe kicked the door closed, grabbed her leg, and pulled her down as the guns opened up.

They were solid projectile weapons, and rounds smashed through the walls, glass and masonry shattering, bullets whining up from the stonework.

Wolfe lay flat, trying to hold Ariadne. "The lights," he shouted. "Where's the cutoff switch for the lights?"

Ariadne didn't answer, struggling in blind panic, kicking, clawing, trying to get away. She kneed him, he gasped in pain, and she scrambled up, trying to run anywhere, nowhere.

The guns crashed once more. There were three fist-sized holes in Ariadne Penruddock's back, green turning black as the woman skidded to her knees, then collapsed facedown. Joshua was reflexively half-up; the gunmen sent more rounds chattering through the house, and he went down again.

Joshua rolled on his back, pulling the now-futile blaster as the lifters made two more passes, bullets tearing the night apart.

The door above him tore away, and there was a glow from the still-burning path lights.

Now it's over, he thought. Now they come in with grenades and finish it.

But the lighters put on full power and were gone. Joshua barely heard the sound of their receding engines through the ringing in his ears.

He got shakily to his feet.

Dust hazed the foyer, and he had the iron taste of blood in his mouth. He saw movement, and belatedly, his gun was in his hand. Judge Penruddock staggered toward him. His hand was clasped over one arm, trying to stop the pulsing blood. His lips moved soundlessly.

Joshua heard a cracking, and Penruddock's trophy, legs splintered from the bullets, crashed down onto the judge. Joshua dove away, rolling, down the hall, as the beast smashed into pieces.

Then there was silence.

He went back to the foyer.

Malcolm Penruddock's body was crushed under the shattered monster, except for one hand and forearm. It twitched and was still.

Wolfe went to Ariadne Penruddock's body. He didn't turn it over. He didn't want to see her face.

He reached down, touched her hand, then went quickly out of the house and around the side, away from the road, the light, and the building scream of sirens.

* CHAPTER EIGHT *

"You were there when they slotted them?" Cisco asked.

Wolfe nodded.

"How'd you get out? They have their best cops, such as they are, on it. Penruddock was a big name, and so was his wife."

Wolfe just looked at Cisco.

The FI man shrugged. "All right. I didn't think you'd tell me. Did you leave any trail at all?"

"Not much of one," Wolfe said. "I was moving under my real name, but the only link would be two com calls, one to Penruddock's house, one back to me."

"The cops aren't even looking for a Mister Inside. But I'll make sure you stay clean."

"What's the best theory?"

"Their murder squad is going on the assumption that one of Penruddock's old partners in corruption was holding a grudge and waited until now to settle it."

"Ten years after the war, after he retires? That's thin."

"That's all they've got."

"What about the triggermen?"

"Import talent. There was a freighter that landed two days earlier, had an open exit clearance, and lifted twelve minutes after the first reports of gunfire came in. No guns, no gunnies, no aircraft found so far, so everything must've gotten back aboard that ship."

"What registry?"

"Micked. The ship came in with recognition numbers from a Halliday Line freighter that we have a positive location for on the other side of the galaxy. As for its papers," Cisco went on, "Mandodari isn't too particular about who lands there these days."

"A pretty goddamned pro touch on somebody who's been retired as long as the judge has. If he was telling me the truth," Wolfe said.

"Okay. There's another theory. Khodyan had friends who are doing paybacks."

Wolfe snorted and didn't bother answering.

"It didn't fly for me, either," Cisco agreed. "Try another one. His wife. Any angles there? Word is she led a pretty spectacular life."

"No," Wolfe said. "It has to be the Lumina." He leaned forward. "Cisco. *Who else is in the field? I've got to know!*"

Cisco shook his head. "I don't know. I swear, Joshua, I'm not lying to you."

His gaze was bland, sincere.

* * *

"Are we screened?" The on-screen Ben Greet glanced around as if he could somehow see any taps.

"Now, Ben, that's your problem, not mine. I can guarantee the com link is sealed on this end. I'm using the Sector Marshal's own set."

Wolfe was lying. He was linked to Platte on one of Cisco's secure coms.

"What do you need, Joshua? You didn't leave any loose ends here when you left, did you? I don't have the . . . the things you gave me anymore."

"Not interested in those. What I want to know is everything you have on Sutro. The fence that was going to meet Innokenty Khodyan."

The pickup was good enough for Wolfe to see sweat bead the resort owner's forehead.

"Joshua, I swear, I don't know anything at all. And even if I did, you know I couldn't tell you anything. I've got to stay known as a man who can keep it buttoned."

"Ben, talk to me. I don't want to have to come all the way to Platte and have this conversation again."

Wolfe let the silence linger and held Greet's eyes. The man winced as if he'd been struck.

"All right. I've met him four times. Big man. Might have been a fighter once. Let himself get sloppy. He told me once he was going to get back in shape as soon as he had the energy. Black hair, don't remember the color of his eyes; he had a beard this last time, black, going gray. I'd guess he's in his early fifties.

"He speaks like he has a bit of education but sometimes slips into street talk. Generally travels with half a dozen guards. He has his own ship. I don't know where it's registered."

"Is Sutro his real name?"

"It's the only one I've ever heard him use. He or any of his ... clients."

"Where's he out of?"

Greet's expression slipped for an instant, and the complacency showed. "Now, that I don't know, and I haven't inquired. Joshua, I know what the most idle curiosity can cost, remember?"

"What happened when he arrived this last time?"

"Now, that is interesting," Greet said, a note of animation coming into his voice. "He ported where you did, about a day later, had his own lifter, and came straight on in without notification.

"He found out about you—don't look at me that way. I said I didn't know who you were, just some kind of FI warrant hunter. Anyway, he heard the news and flitted like a stripe-assed ape within the hour. He seemed really unhappy, too."

"Go back to the other times you met him. Does he illicit buy anything, or is it just jewelry?"

"He'll deal in anything that's high-dollar and easily transportable. I've known him to handle art, minerals, company certificates. He's clean, slick, pays twenty-five percent of the legal price, which is better than most. I've heard he gets away with it by preselling what he buys—or else being the go-between for commissioned 'work.' "

Wolfe found that interesting, but his face showed nothing. "What about his pleasures? Whores? Drugs? Liquor?"

"He'll tumble a dox as long as he can pretend he's not paying for it directly. He drinks a bit. No drugs. His main vice is gambling. That's one reason he likes Yoruba, because my games are straight."

"How does he pay his bills? Or do you comp him like you did me?"

"Of course not. He pays his way like any other member of the profession. Hold on. I'll call his account up."

Greet stepped off-screen, was gone for some minutes, then came back. "Uses a standard debit card on a draw account."

"What bank?"

"Numbered only."

"Give it to me."

"Joshua . . ."

"Come on, Greet."

Greet heaved a reluctant sigh. "You're recording this, I know. Here it comes."

His off-screen hand tapped a keyboard, and numbers scrolled across Joshua's screen.

"I'll save you some work, Joshua. But please don't ask me about Sutro, not ever again. And I don't think you'd better come back to Yoruba."

Joshua didn't respond.

"The card was issued on some planet called Rialto. I don't know anything about it at all. That's all I've got."

"Thanks, Ben. I'll leave you in peace. For now. But one thing. Don't even think about tipping Sutro. He's a maybe, but I'm certain."

Joshua touched the sensor. The connection must have blanked on Greet's end first, because before the image broke up, Joshua saw the fat man's face pucker in a frenzy of rage as he spit into the pickup.

The great house teetered in its abandon like an archaic top hat that had been set upon by mice and small boys. It was back from the road, closed off by a sagging and rusted razor-wire fence. There was a large, new stainless-steel cylinder sticking up out of the ground that was the input side of a pneumatic delivery system.

The gate sagged on its hinges. Wolfe eased through and went up the cracked and overgrown walk. Grass grew thick around the main building, and the trees were long unpruned, broken branches caressing the ground. It had gotten worse since the last time Joshua had been there.

The house looked tired, gray, as if its date with demolition contractors had been broken and never remade, and now it just waited, knowing time could do no more, and the final collapse would be welcome.

Wolfe touched a com sensor. It was ten minutes before the box crackled.

"Go away." The voice sounded as cracked and old as the house it came from.

"Mister Davout? This is Joshua Wolfe. I need some help."

Another long silence.

"Wolfe? Commander Wolfe?"

Joshua took a deep breath. "That's right."

"I'm sorry. Very sorry. There's been some young vandals. I didn't mean to be rude. Come right in."

There was a *clack* as the door auto-unlocked and swung open.

Wolfe smelled damp, decay, rot and entered. The house's central hallway was stacked with neatly bundled and tied newscoms reaching high over Wolfe's head. The door to a front room stood open. It was almost full of boxes. Wolfe looked into one. It held unopened music-fiche shipping containers.

"I'm upstairs, Commander. Be careful. I've added some new precautions."

Wolfe went down the hall toward the stairs. Another room he passed was stacked high with the gadgets of the moment from the last ten years in their original packaging.

His stomach churned as he caught the reek from the kitchen. It had been a long time since it had seen a scrub unit or, for that matter, cooked a meal. He saw a sink stacked high with dishes, green and black mold spilling over the stainless basins toward the floor. To one side were row after row of freezer units and, beside them, the interior outlet of the pneumo-tube.

The stairs were a tunnel of baled papers arching close overhead, and Wolfe had to turn sideways to go up them. He moved very slowly, hearing the creak of the uncertain bales and seeing every now and then bright steel wire carefully laid where the careless would be certain to step and bring tons of paper tumbling down.

He didn't look in any of the rooms on the second floor but went up to the top floor.

That had once been a single room, probably a conservatory, since there were double-panel glass squares overhead that had been sloppily painted black. The room had been divided and divided again by more baled papers, except those papers came from the huge, if elderly, superspeed printer.

Waiting was a small man who, like his house, smelled of decay. He wore a tattered set of coveralls and slippers.

"You're not in uniform," Davout said in relief.

Wolfe frowned in puzzlement.

"If you had any bad news about my brother," the little man explained, "you would have come in uniform. And there would have been a doctor or priest. That's the way they always do it."

Davout's brother had been a civilian com tech on a world that had been one of the first seized by the Al'ar when the war had started. Like Joshua's parents, he'd been interned. But unlike them, there'd been no confirmation as to his fate. It had merely been missing . . . missing . . . missing, presumed dead . . . and then, when all the prison worlds had been fine-combed, the flat report: DECEASED.

Davout had never believed any of the reports, and so he'd kept everything from the day he'd heard of his brother's capture, sure that one day, one hour, the man would stride up the walk and want to know what had happened while he was away.

"So how is the war going? Never mind. You don't have to tell me. Well, well enough, or else I wouldn't be able to reach out to as many worlds as I can. Sit down, Commander, sit down. I'll make tea."

Davout picked up a stack of microfiches from a rickety chair, looked about helplessly for a place to put them, and finally set them on the floor. Joshua sat awkwardly. Davout left the cubicle they were in and went into another, where Joshua could see a tiny heating plate and micro-oven. Another cubicle beside it held a chemical toilet that from the smell Davout had forgotten to recycle for a while.

All that was in the paper-walled cubicle was the chair Wolfe sat in, a second torn office chair, a stained canvas cot, and the console that had brought him there. It was an amazing assemblage of electronics, none appearing less than five years old, most still anodized in various mil-spec shades of dullness.

"You know, Commander," Davout's voice came. "When this war ends, I think we should consider war crimes trials for the Al'ar. I mean, it's just not right for them to treat people the way they do.

"Don't you agree?"

Joshua made a noncommittal noise, almost felt like crying. Once, three years before, he'd tried to tell Davout, tried to show him. The little man had stared as if Wolfe had begun speaking in a completely unknown tongue. He'd waited until Wolfe had stammered into silence, then had continued their conversation where Wolfe had so rudely interrupted it.

Davout came out, cautiously balancing two mismatched dirty cups holding a dark substance.

"If you want milk or sugar, I'll have to go belowstairs," he said. "I don't partake, as you know, so I keep forgetting my manners and keep some on hand."

"That's fine, Mister Davout."

"So what brings you this time? You know, I don't ever think I've really thanked you for what you're doing for me. I mean, I know who you work for . . ." Davout looked cagily at Wolfe through thick, tangled eyebrows. "You don't need to tell me. I've read about you intelligence operatives. I'm glad you trust me enough to help with your projects. It keeps me from . . . thinking too much. About things.

"I just hope I'm doing my share to win the war."

Wolfe coughed, clearing his throat. "This time it should be easy, Mister Davout."

"Go ahead." Davout picked up a v-helmet and held it ready. "Oh, I've forgotten to tell you something. I've made a new acquisition." He pointed to a second helmet half-hidden behind a pile of paper. "If you want to ride along, you're welcome."

Wolfe set the cup down, walked over, and got the helmet. It was even older than the one Davout held and, like the little man's, had been extensively modified, the jerry-rigged modifications e-taped or glued in place.

Wolfe pulled out the rubber bands that retracted the headphones, put the helmet on, and slid the black visor over his face. He started as something crawled across his throat, then realized it was the helmet's microphone.

"There we are," Davout's voice came. "Now, what do we need?"

"A planet named Rialto. I don't know where it is, what it is. But I need to find out something about its banks."

"Ah."

The universe spun around Wolfe, a whirl of figures, starcharts, stardrive blur that could only be a latent personal memory, more figures. Wolfe's stomach came up, and he pulled the helmet off.

Davout must have sensed something, because he

turned from his place at the console and lifted his own visor. "Is something the matter?"

"It's been too long since I did this," Joshua said truthfully. "A little vertigo."

"Oh." Davout was disappointed. "It's always better to have someone along. It's sort of like—like having a friend. But never mind. Let me see what there is to see."

"Now, here we are. Rialto, more or less Earth type—ah hah, I can see why you mentioned banks. I read: 'Rialto's biggest source of income is its banks. They are privately chartered, but with the full encouragement of the government behind them, and all transactions are completely secret, as are depositors and all other financial data. All attempts by Federation law enforcement have failed to secure any degree of cooperation, and all known attempts to penetrate the so-called golden veil of Rialto have failed; hence, the planet is a well-known monetary sanctuary for criminals, tax evaders, and others who prefer that their financial business remain secret.' Mercy. How can they do something like that? Don't they know there's a war on?"

"So we're screwed?"

"Hmmph. Make yourself some more tea, Commander."

"Oh, my. That's cute. That's very cute. They have a wonderful little booby trap set up so that anybody who tries to crawl his way in using an ANON password gets back blasted.

"Very sexy," Davout said admiringly. "So let's try another way."

"Damn! Pardon, Commander. But a man living by himself gets careless about his language."

"What's going on?" Wolfe was getting a little bleary. He'd been sitting in the chair, and occasionally on the cot, for six straight hours with no breaks other than what Davout considered tea and a visit to the redolent toilet.

"I tried another way in and got my paws slapped," Davout said. "Hmm. This may take a little thought."

"Ah hah, ha hah, ha hah," Davout crooned. "You didn't even see me slip past the gate, now, did you?"

"You're in."

"I'm in. Isn't it a good thing that we're honest people? We could be very rich if we weren't.

"Now, what, or who, did you want to know about? Rialto is an open ledger, as their bankers might say."

"That's the second problem. All I have is a single name. Sutro. Spelled like it sounds. It's a person, male. I'm not sure if he uses or even has a second name. It would be an active account, very active, with lots of credits going in and out. The only action I know of for sure would be a bill paid to an account called YORUBA or possibly BEN GREET."

"Very good, very good. That's what I like about you, Commander. You never come to me with the easy stuff."

* * *

"Sutro, Sutro, there you are."

As Davout spoke, the printer beside him clicked, and sheets of paper spat out.

Wolfe started up from his drowse. It was after midnight, and Davout hadn't said anything at all for the last hour and a half.

"We now have everything there is to know about your Mister Sutro. My, but he's rich. Spends it, too."

"What's his home world? Do you have that?"

"I have everything he had to file with the bankers to set up his call account." Davout lifted the helmet off. "Rialto, it appears, is very sensitive about exposing themselves to any risk, so I have quite an extensive dossier on Mister Sutro, which you'll be holding in about five minutes. But to end the suspense, his home world is a place called Trinité. If you want—"

"I'm familiar with it—at least where it is. Mister Davout, you're a hell of a guy. I can't say how grateful I am."

The little man smiled shyly. "Thank you, Commander. Thank you." He was silent for a time. Wolfe waited, knowing he was trying to find the courage to ask something. Finally:

"You said I've helped you. Would it be out of place for me to ask for a favor?"

"Anything I can do."

"I know there's a thousand, maybe a million like me, who've got family held by the Al'ar. But would you mind, would it be possible, for you to see if you can learn something? I mean, I don't know what kind of connections you Intelligence people have behind the Al'ar lines, but is there anything you could find out?"

The little man's eyes were pleading, desperate.

"Joshua, this stinks on ice." Sector Marshal Achebe held the microfiche as if it belonged in a fume cabinet.

"It's a perfectly legitimate complaint," Wolfe said, trying to suppress a grin.

"Legitimate, maybe. But don't you think there's something somewhat irregular when a complaint gets filed about some resident of the planet of Trinité, by name of Sutro, on a charge of conspiracy to violate Federation statutes up to and including murder and further alleges that this Sutro also conspired to conceal his part in said crimes and further is likely to commit even more heinous crimes if not brought to the bar immediately?"

"What's wrong with that?"

"It reeketh when the person filing said complaint happens to be a warrant hunter named Joshua Wolfe," Achebe complained. "Now what are you going to do? Go out and serve your own warrant?"

"Of course."

"Samedi with a new derby," Achebe swore. "Are you also going to post a reward?"

"Nope. Thought that might be a little much."

"Joshua, Joshua. Why?"

Wolfe's smile vanished. "Because I might run into some trouble with whatever passes for law on Trinité. I'd like to have some cover."

"You know this Sutro doesn't have any record with the Federation? At least nothing I could find."

"I know. That's another reason for the complaint."

"Trinité's quite a planet."

"Never been there."

"Let's say it's got a *lot* of gold. I'm glad it's not in my sector. The people there seem to think they can do pretty much what they want and buy off any complaints afterward."

"Are they right?"

"Damned close," Achebe admitted. "Which brings up my last question. If the shit hits the fan, what do you think I'll be able to do to help?"

"Send flowers, maybe."

Achebe sighed in relief. "Okay. I'll approve and E-post it. I assume you don't want any real circulation but just want it there for the record.

"I was afraid you'd slipped a notch and thought the law in the Outlaw Worlds maybe was going to actually be able to do something."

"I know better than that, Jagua."

"You have time for a drink? Might be your last, you know."

"With a cheery invite like that, how could I refuse?"

"So you're alive."

"Alive? I do not know if that is the proper concept. All systems are locked into green. All circuitry is performing better than before I was refitted, and my sensors advise that all parts of me are as good as or better than when I was first launched. Thank you."

Joshua was astonished.

"Thank you?"

"My programmer said you would be startled," the ship went on. *"She said a bit of a personality was*

needed. I have no computation on the value of her be-lief."

Joshua chuckled. "All right. It's nice to have you back, if your circuits can now interpret that. I could have used your services a couple of times in the last month. Is everything go?"

"Affirmative. Destination tape running. Tower clearance granted. At your command."

"Let's do it."

The *Grayle* shuddered, came off the shipyard ways, hovered down a solid-painted line to a lift point, then rose still higher, canted to near vertical, and screamed up off Carlton VI.

The unobtrusive man wearing dark, sober clothing put his binocs back in their case and started unhurriedly toward the com booth at the back of the observation deck.

* CHAPTER NINE *

The first Al'ar struck the boy from behind, sending him sprawling. Joshua, as taught, tucked and rolled, coming up as the second Al'ar youth flashed a hand across the boy's stomach, a seeming touch that made Joshua scream in agony and stumble back.

The third was maneuvering to get behind him, and Joshua spun kicked, his boot crashing into the Al'ar's thigh. The alien fell but made no sound, although his hood flared wide in pain and both hands grasped his leg.

The first came in once more, thin white arm darting out like a pointer, touching Joshua's wrist and sending pain burning up his arm.

Joshua had the alley wall at his back, and he waited, trying to keep tears from welling and blinding him.

The Al'ar attacked again, and Joshua ducked his head to the side and sent a hammer strike into the Al'ar's chest. The alien squealed and fell, and one of his friends dragged him back. The other two hesitated, then grabbed the third by the shoulders and were gone into the evening mist.

Joshua fought pain, fought collapse.

Another Al'ar moved out of the darkness.

"You fought well," he said. "For a groundworm."

That was one of the Al'ar terms for terrestrials.

"To the mud with you," Joshua managed. "If you wish to share what your friends found, you have but to ask."

"I desire no self-proving this evening," the Al'ar said. Joshua only half understood his words. His family had been stationed on Sauros for only three E-months, and he was still being tutored.

"Then remove your worthless self from my way." Joshua limped forward.

"I will help you," the Al'ar said, seemingly undisturbed by the insults. He stepped forward, and Joshua managed a guard stance.

"You need not fear me. I have spoken my intent."

Joshua hesitated, then, for an unknown reason, let the Al'ar lift his arm around his neck. All the Al'ar appeared emaciated but were able to lift far more than most terrestrials—another mystery unanswered.

"I live—"

"I know your burrow," the Al'ar said. "You are the hatchling of the One Who Speaks for All Groundlings." Astonishingly, the Al'ar continued in strangely accented Terran: "Your word is 'Ambassador'?"

Joshua stopped in his tracks. "You speak my language! No one has ever done that."

"There are a few of us who are . . . weird? No, aberrant. It is not thought good to ... reduce yourself and speak like a Lesser One."

"Thank you for very little. I will not embarrass you any more," Joshua said. "I must learn your words better, anyway."

The Al'ar made no response, and they limped on.

"I was interested seeing the way you fought," the Al'ar said. "I have never seen a groundworm do that."

"It has the name of—" Joshua was forced back into Terran. "—tae kwan do." Then he returned to Al'ar. "It is a discipline you must work at. My father is a master, and when I learned all he had, he found one who was his master to teach me more."

"Perhaps you should learn our ways of fighting. They are very deadly. Those hatchlings were but toying with you. If they had learned their skills well or intended real harm, you would not be on this plane. So I would say our ways are better than your tae kwan do."

"Who would teach me?"

"Perhaps," the Al'ar said, "I might. If I wished."

Joshua stared at the alien but decided not to question him.

"Why," Joshua asked, "did they attack me?"

"Because they were curious."

"Three of them against one? And hitting me from behind?"

The Al'ar turned his snakelike head toward the boy. "But of course," he said, and Joshua thought he distinguished surprise. "Would you have us fight one at a time from the front? That way dictates loss. Pain."

"That is what we call—" Joshua hunted for the word, couldn't find it in Al'ar, and switched to Terran. "—a coward."

"That is a word I have seen but do not understand."

"We do not respect those who lack courage to fight—" Again there was no Al'ar word, so he returned to Terran. "—fairly."

"I think my mind can hear that last word and know it. We have our customs, you have yours."

"So why are you helping me?"

There was a silence.

"I do not know," the Al'ar said finally. "Sometimes I think I am mad."

"You are the first Al'ar who has been anything other than a . . . a worm turd to me."

"As I said, there are those who think me mad. But you do not have my name. You may call me Taen. Perhaps that explains my behavior, for it would be, in your language, the One Who Stands Aside and Wonders."

Joshua's eyes opened, and the ship noticed and brought the lights up slightly. He lay without moving for a while.

"Now why," he mused, "didn't that dream bother me?"

After a while his eyes closed, his breathing became regular, and the ship, after the programmed time, dimmed the lights.

* * *

The *Grayle* came in on a lazy braking orbit, the ship circling Trinité three times before closing on the main island of Morne-des-Esses, giving Wolfe a chance to turn computer images into reality.

Trinité was mostly water and islands, with two desert landmasses near the equator that cut the tidal action of the triple moons and made the equatorial islands habitable and the shallow seas around them navigable. North and south of the continents the waves rolled ceaselessly, hammering at the few rocky skerries that still jutted from the boiling seas.

Morne-des-Esses curled like a protective snake around half a hundred tiny islets. The world's capital and only real city, Diamant, sat on Morne-des-Esses's largest bay, its streets twisting up the steep hills that ran almost to the water's edge.

"I have Trinité Control on-line. Need input."

"Patch 'em through," a speaker went on. "Trinité Control, what's your problem?"

"Negative problem," the voice said, and Wolfe wondered why it was obligatory for all pilots and navigation points, human or roboticized, to drawl as if there were all the time in the world. *"We have two landing options, as your ship was advised. One is Wule, conventional spaceport, all facilities, on land. The other is Diamant Port, just offshore from the city. Your charts should indicate details. Ships berth like watercraft at buoys, com links available at buoy head, water taxis available on call or signal.*

"Wule Port is ten credits a day, Diamant fifty. Have you reached a decision?"

"That's affirm, Trinité Control. We'll take Diamant."

*"Understood. Turning you over to Diamant
Subcontrol."*

"Take it on in," Wolfe said. "Try to land like a rich
bitch's yacht. Blow spray in somebody's face or something."

"Assumption: That is not an order," the ship said.
"You are making a joke."

"Thank you for informing me."

The ship lowered into the water like a suspicious ma-
tron into a bathtub, and Wolfe heard hissing through the
outside mikes as the atmosphere-seared hull sent steam
boiling. On secondary drive the ship cruised into the
harbor and down a row of buoys, some with yachts,
others with starcraft moored to them. It found the assigned buoy, and mag-grapples shot out.

*"Diamant Subcontrol advised there are anchors
available for an additional fee, which they recommend
in the event of a storm. Should I signal for them? I have
no familiarity with such gear."*

"Disregard. They're getting enough of our credits as
is. Instructions: If I am not in the ship and a storm does
blow up, take whatever measures are necessary to keep
yourself safe, including lifting off."

"Understood. We are now landed."

Artificial gravity went off, and Wolfe's inner ear
complained slightly. The ship moved gently to wave-
rhythm.

"Open up and let's see what we've got," Wolfe said.

The ship opened the lock and slid the retractable
loading platform below it. Joshua walked out onto it.
He was about two feet above the ocean.

The water was blue, calm, peaceful, and the sun glared white on the rooftops of Diamant. A breeze ruffled the water like a mother's fingers, then passed on. It was a day, and a world, that said that nothing much mattered beyond the moment.

"Hey, Cap'n!" The voice came from a gaily painted boat that to Joshua's surprise looked as if it were built of wood. Its owner had close-cropped hair and freckles and looked about fourteen. She was slim-built and wore shorts and a baggy exercise shirt with LIBANOS WATER TAXIS on it.

"You need to go ashore?"

"In a bit."

The young woman expertly gunned her boat toward the *Grayle*'s platform, reversed the drive, and let it drift up until a fender touched the ship.

"What's a bit? If you're coming now, fine. Otherwise I'll come back on my next run."

Joshua didn't answer; he walked back into the ship, touched a blank wall, and took coins from the drawer that slotted out. He went back out.

"What's your hourly?"

"Two credits." The girl grinned. "More if I think you're good for it."

Joshua sent the coins spinning through the air, reflections bouncing off the water. The girl caught them one-handed and made them disappear.

"I'm yours for . . . two hours. What do you want? The grand tour?"

"As soon as customs comes out to clear me."

The girl laughed raucously. "Captain, there isn't any customs on Trinité. They've already checked your credit balance before they let you land, especially here in the harbor. If you're solvent, you're welcome. I hope you're not carrying anything real contagious. My shots aren't up to date."

"Healthy as two horses. You are . . . ?"

"You can call me Thetis."

Joshua grinned. "You pick that yourself, or did somebody with a crystal ball come up with it?"

"My grandfather gave it to me. Said he never liked what I'd been birth-named with." She shrugged. "I don't even remember my other name now."

"My name's Joshua Wolfe. Hang on while I grab a couple of things."

The *Grayle*'s lock hissed shut behind Joshua, and the platform retracted as soon as he'd stepped into Thetis's boat. He wore white trousers, deck shoes, a light green shirt, and a coarsely woven silk windbreaker. He did not appear armed.

"Where to?"

"Like you said, the grand tour. I'd like to get an idea of what the island's like. Never been here before."

Thetis put the boat into drive and sent it hissing away, its wake purling white. The boat looked very old-fashioned, about eighteen feet long with a covered fore-deck, a glass windshield, and three rows of seats. The hull was lacquered, and the detail was gleaming white.

"Is this real wood?"

"It is," the girl said. "Hand-laid by Granddad, but now I'm the one who's got to keep it afloat. Keeps me busy, but I don't mind. Wood feels different than resin or even metal. I wouldn't trade *Dolphin* for anything."

Without a noticeable pause she asked, "You on vacation?"

"Why else would anybody come here?"

"Lots of reasons," Thetis said.

"Such as?"

The girl looked at him, then away at the harbor. "My grandfather said, when he turned the boat over to me, never to ask the customers more than they want to say and tell 'em even less."

"Your grandfather sounds like he's been around."

"And then some. He mostly raised me. He said I didn't need to go to Diamant's schools as long as I passed his teachings. I guess I did all right."

"Who was Thetis's father?"

"Ask me a hard one. Nereus. His folks were Pontus and Gaea."

"Where are your forty-nine sisters?"

The grin vanished from the girl's lips.

"They didn't live through the war," she said tonelessly. "Any more'n my mother and father did. My grandfather tracked me down in a crèche."

"Sorry," Joshua said, apologizing. "I lost my own folks when the war started."

The girl nodded but didn't respond. After a moment: "Diamant," she began, "has about fifty thousand legal residents, maybe sixty now. There's about double that who're visitors, or who have job permits, or who're just here without bothering anybody. The island's industries are tourism, fishing—"

"I read the Baedeker coming in," Joshua interrupted. "How many casinos does Diamant have now?"

The girl turned. "Now I've got your ID. You didn't

look like a banker on the run or somebody here to toast his toes. You a pro or just somebody who likes the action?"

"Only a man who's interested in the sporting life."

"You just gave me the rest of it," she said with satisfaction. "Granddad says that anybody who's careful of what he says about gaming generally is somebody who'll make you a bet he can make the jack of diamonds jump out of the deck and piddle in your ear, and you'd best not play with him unless you want a real wet ear.

"We've got five big casinos, plus there's who knows how many quiet games or even full-scale joints. There's enough action to keep anybody happy. You see all those islands?" She pointed out away from the harbor. "Those are all private. Could be anything on any of them. The Diamant Council doesn't care much once somebody buys or leases them. If there's complaints or troubles, they'll send somebody out to see what's going on and levy a fine if it's real bad."

"Do gamblers have to register?"

"They're supposed to. But nobody bothers. What kind of gaming you looking for?"

"Thetis, anybody ever tell you don't act like—what, fourteen?"

"Fifteen next month. Thanks, mister. Nobody with a sure fix on anything wants to be a kid any longer than she has to, right?"

Joshua inclined his head in agreement. "You ever hear of anybody named Sutro? He's supposedly a resident."

"Nope. But I don't ask much, either."

Joshua took a bill from his pocket, folded it, and tucked it in the girl's coverall. She looked down into the pocket and looked surprised.

"That's just for asking?"

"It is. But ask quietly."

"Mister Wolfe, I don't do *anything* noisily. It doesn't pay to attract attention unless you want to. I'll find out and get back to you.

"You still want the tour?"

"I paid for it, I'm going to get it," Joshua said, and lounged back on the brightly colored canvas seat.

The girl looked at him speculatively, then went on with her description of the scenic wonders of Morne-des-Esses.

"Here," Thetis said as Joshua stepped out of the boat onto the dock, and handed him what appeared to be a thick calling card. "Press on the little boat symbol if you need transportation, and that'll buzz me. Twenty-four-hour call." Without waiting for a response, she tapped the drive into gear and shot away.

Joshua turned to the gangplank and stretched like a great cat in the sun, then went up the cleated ramp.

A man who, with his baggy multistriped pants and cotton shirt that reaffirmed that he really was on TRINITÉ, SO BEAUTIFUL GOD SHOULD HAVE QUIT HERE, could only be a tourist was staring into the back end of an elaborate camera. The camera sat on a tripod of absurdly thin and shiny metal that should never have supported its weight.

The camera was focused on a woman at the edge of

the dock. She was some years younger than the man and perhaps half again his weight.

Joshua looked over the man's shoulder curiously. The camera's rear showed an exact duplicate of the harbor in front of them. The man held a small pointer and, one by one, eliminated all the anchored ships. To one side of the frame a large sailing yacht was entering the harbor. The man touched the pointer to it and moved the image closer to the center of the screen. He saw Joshua's shadow and turned.

"Morning, friend. Isn't this the way it's supposed to be?"

"Damned if I know," Joshua said. "I didn't know there was any right or wrong way for scenery."

"Sure there is. The man who teaches the class I take said that the object of attention—that's my wife, Dorena—should be at the lower third of the picture. Then the eye should move upward, to the right, which is why I moved that boat where I did. Then the eye goes left again, to that big building up on the hill that looks like a toadstool, whatever it is—"

"That's one of the casinos."

"—and that's what makes good composition. Right?"

"Guess so. What do you do next?"

"Seal the image, then print it."

"One thing you might want to do," Joshua suggested, "is move that lamp standard that's growing out of your wife's head."

"Well, I'll be . . ." The man laughed at himself, obliterated the pole, then touched buttons, and a print obediently slid out the base of the camera. "C'mere, hon.

Meet the man who just kept me from doing it dumb again. Mister . . ."

"Wolfe. Joshua."

"I'm Arabo Hofei. We just came down yesterday on the *Darod*. We'll be here for two weeks and enjoying every minute of it. I saw you come in from that starship anchored out there. Is it yours?"

"It is."

The man shook his head. "Wish I could figure out a way to make those kind of credits. But then, some of us are meant to have it and some of us meant not, right, Dorena?"

"We do all right," the woman said. "Besides, what would we do with a big hulk like that? Keep it on our balcony? I imagine docking fees must be astronomical."

Joshua laughed, and after a moment the woman decided she'd just been clever and joined in. She suddenly broke off, looking behind her.

Two unobtrusive men wearing dark sober clothing walked past. Their faces were calm, and their low conversation was of serious matters most likely beyond this world's concern.

"Now, don't those two look like they're having a swell time," she said a bit loudly—loudly enough for one of the men to look at her calmly, then turn his attention away. Dorena blushed.

"I didn't *mean* to be overheard," she almost whispered. "Wonder who they are."

"Chi something, I think," her husband said.

"Chitet," Joshua added.

"What are they? Some kind of priests?"

"Sort of," Arabo said. "I read something about them

once. They're like a cult, aren't they? Don't believe in emotions or things like that, right?"

"Pretty much," Joshua said. "They're an old group. Men, women, children. They pretty much keep to themselves. They have half a dozen, maybe more worlds of their own.

"There's a story that three or four hundred years ago they planned a coup against the Federation. They thought they were entitled to run things because they never let emotion get in the way. They thought they could take a few key posts, or so the story goes, and the Federation would shrug, realize the Chitet were the best possible governors, and let what'd happened go on.

"The coup never came off. The story says that at the last minute their leaders ran probability studies and decided they had only a fifty-fifty chance and called it off.

"Supposedly the authorities arrested their leadership but couldn't get anyone to talk. Since there hadn't been any bodies in the street or government houses blown up, the Chitet weren't proscribed.

"But that was a long time ago. Since they're like you said, priding themselves on always using pure logic, they're considered pretty respectable, and a lot of businesses, even governments, use them for comptrollers, auditors, and things like that."

"Pretty good, Joshua," Arabo said admiringly. "You rattled that off like you were reading it from a screen. What are you, some kind of professor?"

"When you're between stars," Joshua said, "there isn't much else to do but read. Sorry. I guess I did sound a little pompous."

"Nothing wrong with that," Dorena said. "Lord

knows we could all do with more learning than what we have." She leaned close to Arabo, whispered something, then giggled. Arabo chuckled.

Joshua lifted an eyebrow.

"My wife wondered if these Chitet, uh, make love."

"I guess they do," Wolfe said. "There's supposed to be a lot of them."

"I knew *nobody* could stay sobersided all the time," Dorena said. "We're going out on the glass-bottom boat, Mister Wolfe. You want to go with us?"

"No, thanks," Joshua said. "I just grounded and want to look around."

The Hofeis gathered their photographic gear, and Joshua moved on toward the road that led to the big mushroom-shaped building on the hill.

In the daytime, the Casino d'Or was cheap-looking, smelling of broken promises and stale perfume, like all whores in sunlight. There were only a handful of people on the tables trying to spend fast enough to catch up with their fleeing dreams.

Joshua leaned against a wall, picking out the various games. A beefy man wearing a tunic tailored to hide a gun drifted up and pretended interest in a gaming machine a few feet away.

Joshua walked over to him.

"You work here." It was a statement, not a question.

After a moment the man moved his head a trifle vertically.

"I'm looking for a friend of mine by the name of Sutro. Since he likes to gamble, I thought you might be familiar with him."

The man's dead eyes gazed at Joshua.

Wolfe took out a bill, folded it, and held it out. The man didn't take the note, nor did he respond. Joshua put the bill away.

"My apologies, friend. I thought you were sentient," he said, and started for the exit.

* CHAPTER TEN *

Joshua jerked back from the display as an Al'ar glared at him.

Around the holograph, words formed:

**THE
SECRETS
OF THE
AL'AR**

**Their Secret Weapons!
Their Covert Society!
Their Hidden Ways!
Their Murderous Skills!
Their Perverted Culture!**

. . . which was coming very soon, less than two E-months away, to Morne-des-Esses, fresh from triumphs on Worlds A, B, C, and so on, and Joshua would be well advised to buy his tickets in advance, for the demand for this Educational Opportunity would be Most Great . . .

"Never underestimate the absolute goddamned stupidity," Joshua began in some disgust, about to punch out of *New and Notable on Trinité* but he was interrupted.

"We have visitors," the ship announced. *"It is the girl Thetis and an old man. Shall I extend the loading platform?"*

"Go ahead." Joshua got up, started for the lock, then turned aside, opened the arms cabinet, and tucked a small blaster in his waistband at the small of his back.

"Give me a visual."

He saw Thetis and a fierce-looking old man with archaic sideburns that ran up into a walrus mustache that bristled rage. He shrugged.

"Open the port."

It slid open just as the man and girl were getting out of the wooden speedboat.

"Good evening," Wolfe said civilly.

Without preamble: "I'm Jacob Libanos. You gave Thetis quite a bit of money today. I want to talk to you about it."

"I'm listening."

"Trinité can make you think everything's for sale. There's some things that ain't. Thetis is one of them."

The girl looked embarrassed.

"I never thought she was," Joshua said dryly.

The old man studied him for long moments, then nodded. "I'll work on the assumption you're telling the truth. But that isn't the only thing I wanted to talk about. You asked her to look around for somebody named Sutro. You puttin' her to risk?"

"No," Joshua said. "Sutro's a legitimate resident of Diamant, or my sources say he is. I just want to know more about him."

"I'd say you was law, but I checked your ship's registry. Damned odd sort of Federation man'd come out of Carlton VI."

A half smile came and went on Joshua's face. "You've been there."

"I have. It tries just as hard to be decadent as Trinité, but it ain't got the credits to pull it off."

"That's a pretty good description," Joshua agreed. "Come aboard if you want the grand tour."

Libanos nodded and followed Joshua inside.

"Damned big ship," he observed, "for just one man. Or is there crew out of sight?"

"Just me. Ship's automated."

"Heard they'd finally got that down. Haven't been aboard one yet." They went up to the control room. Libanos studied the main station carefully. "Looks pretty easy to run," he observed. "All those damned gauges and readouts that did nothing but beep at you— glad to see them gone. All they did was clutter the mind, anyway. By the time they told you were in trouble, generally you were 'most dead."

"You have your papers?"

"Commercial master, passenger master, the mate buttons to go with 'em. But it's been a long time."

Joshua waited for the man to volunteer his current occupation, but nothing came.

"Let me ask you something, Mister Wolfe."

"Joshua."

"We'll keep it mister for a while, if you don't mind. Thetis . . . or maybe me . . . finds out about your Sutro, what happens then?"

Joshua didn't reply.

"I didn't figure you'd answer that one." Libanos thought for a while, trying to stroke his mustache back into some sort of order.

"All right. We'll do what we can."

Without saying more, he turned toward the port.

Joshua put one hand over the two cards, waited while the bettors made their decisions, then pushed counters across the line.

"*Carte,*" he said, and a card slid across the green baize. He looked at it calmly. "*Non.*"

The banker turned his cards over. He had seven. He took another card. A queen stared haughtily up.

Joshua turned his cards, showing six, and let the croupier's paddle take away more of his counters.

The banker touched the shoe, and Joshua *felt* what would happen.

"*Banco,*" he said.

The banker looked pointedly at the small pile of credits beside Joshua. Wolfe reached into an inner pocket of his formal jacket, took out a small plastic card, spun it across. The banker looked at it, buried surprise, and handed it back.

Two cards whispered out of the shoe to Joshua, to the other man playing, and to the banker.

Joshua, without looking at his hand, flipped his cards over. He held a natural.

The banker lifted the corner of his cards and grimaced. The croupier carefully pushed the large stack of credits across, then ceremoniously moved the shoe to Joshua.

The man who'd been banker stood, bowed, and left the table. Another player slid into his seat.

"Gentlemen," Joshua said, and waited for the bets.

Joshua cashed in his winnings, turned away from the cage, and noticed the beefy man. Joshua nodded politely, stepping around him.

He hesitated, then started for the dinner theater. "If you're going to be one, be a big red one," he said to himself wryly.

The line stretched out the door of the theater almost into one of the main gambling rooms. Joshua saw his photographer friend and wife. They beckoned, and he went over.

"Is the show that good?"

"Supposed to be. Sold out an hour ago."

"Oh, well," Joshua said, putting mock sorrow into his voice. "Guess I'll settle for plain food, then."

"Hang on a second, Mister Wolfe. We've got a whole table reserved," Dorena said. "Whyn't you join us?"

Joshua smiled thanks and joined them in line.

"More wine?" Arabo Hofei said.

Joshua shook his head. "I'll have a drink with the show."

"So what did you think of the meal?"

"All right," Joshua said. "But it seems that places trying to feed your eyes don't pay that much attention to the rest of you."

Arabo laughed loudly. He was a little drunk. A couple at the next table looked over and smiled, pleased to hear someone enjoying himself. "Now isn't *that* the truth," he said.

"It wasn't that bad," Dorena said, "but there sure wasn't very much of it." She patted her stomach with a bit of pride. "I'd be a shadow if I had to eat here every night."

"So what are your plans when the show's over, Joshua?" Hofei had assumed first-name terms before the salad.

"Have a drink at the bar. Maybe go back on the tables. Maybe go for a walk."

"You do a lot of gambling?"

"A bit."

"Would you show me—show us—how that dog-goned red-dog game works? I've always wanted to play it, but it goes so fast, I'm afraid," Dorena said.

"That's the way the dealers want it," Joshua said. "Keep the action going, never let people think, and you end up with a bigger piece. But you don't want to play red-dog."

"Why not?" Arabo asked.

"Because the odds will eat you alive. They're about fourteen to one, plus the house generally takes five percent or so off the top."

"I never understood numbers," Dorena complained. "It just looked like fun."

"Winning is fun. Losing isn't," Joshua said flatly. "If you want, I'll show you—"

He was interrupted by an orchestra fanfare. The dance floor opened like a gigantic clamshell, and dancers spun frenetically as the stage hydraulicked up.

There were acrobats; comedians blue, straight, and robotic; tigers; aquabats; jugglers; horses; giant sloths; singers; musicians; and women. Mostly there were women in every stage from nearly naked to spacesuited, dancing, posing, singing, and talking. Joshua guessed it was a very good show for those who liked that sort of thing.

His eyes kept roving the crowd, trying without luck to pick out a man who might match the description he had of Sutro. Once he saw the two Chitet, now joined by a friend, sitting near the stage, watching as intently as they might observe a spreadsheet run.

One dancer caught everyone's attention. She was small, Afro-Oriental, Joshua thought, with long black hair and a pert figure. For a moment he thought she was nude, then realized she was wearing a bodysuit. Her partner was equally striking: tall, strong-muscled, white, platinum blond. The two of them performed alone with no music other than a metronomelike drum and a swirling synth-tone that might have originated on the Japanese long bamboo flute.

The woman floated, hung, turned, seemingly only to touch the earth or her partner's waiting arms for a moment's rejuvenation before taking off once more.

"How does she *do* that?" Dorena sighed. "I used to dance before I met Arabo and he told me it was all right to eat. But even at my best I never dreamed I could . . ." Her voice trailed away, and she looked momentarily disconsolate. Hofei patted her hand.

The tune ended, and the two dancers took their bows and left the stage.

The next act, a hatchet-throwing comic, complete with blond and brunette barely missed "targets," seemed flat to Joshua and his companions. Joshua slipped a debit card into the table's slot before Arabo could get his out in spite of the man's protests.

They were in the lobby when they heard the woman scream, the scream choked off.

The tall white-blond dancer cowered beside the casino's entrance. His partner, the small Afro-Oriental woman, lay sprawled on the concrete nearby.

There were three men in front of them. Two of them were heavy, hard-faced, half grinning, enjoying their work. The third was thin, average build, expensively dressed. He reached down, jerked the dancer to her feet, snarled something, and drew his hand back.

Joshua was across the lobby and through the door. "I'm sorry, sir. But artists aren't permitted to mingle with the guests."

"Funny man," the small man snapped. "Now butt out or get hurt."

"Sorry," Joshua said, and strolled toward them.

"Take him, Bej."

"Right, Elois," one of the goons said, and started toward Wolfe. His hand went into his pocket and came out with a whip club; he slashed as it sprang open. Wolfe ducked, let the lash go overhead, and rapped the man's elbow with the heel of his hand. The man yelped, dropped the club, and grabbed his crazy bone. Wolfe raked a kick down the front of his leg, crashing onto the arch of his foot, and the man screamed loudly, the scream broken into silence as Wolfe hammer struck the front of his skull.

The second thug came in, hands in a shifted cat stance. Wolfe took the same stance for a moment, ignored the other's feint, blocked the following midsection punch, then snapped his blocking hand up, smashing the goon's face with the back of his wrist, ripping his nose away from the cavity. The man gurgled agony, lost interest, and stumbled away.

The small man Wolfe had heard called Elois was backing away. His hand slid into his jacket and came out with a small nickel-plated gun, lifted as Wolfe's hand blurred to the back of his neck, then darted forward.

A shiny dart of black obsidian protruded from the man's wrist. He let go of the gun, stared at the bubbling blood, said "Oh" in a surprised tone, and sat down on the concrete.

Wolfe stepped over, pulled the knife free, wiped it on the man's jacket, and resheathed it. He paid the short man no further mind but turned to the woman. "You need an escort somewhere?"

The woman smiled shakily and touched a finger to the corner of her mouth, where the bruise was beginning to blossom. "I don't know," she said. "You appear more dangerous than he is."

"No, ma'am," Wolfe said. "I've spent my spleen for at least another week. From now on out I'm a pink pussycat."

The woman hesitated, then said, "All right. If you'd walk me to my lifter."

"My privilege."

The woman gazed at her partner. "Thanks," she said. "Thanks *so* much." The tall blond man shrank back as if she'd struck him.

Joshua looked about, saw the Hofeis staring wide-eyed, waved a farewell, took the woman's arm, and led her away, leaving a crowd gathering around the two sprawled men. It had taken just a few seconds. There was still no sign of security or police.

Joshua concentrated on his breathing: in through the nose, out through the diaphragm. After forty breaths his heartbeat was normal.

"You follow the Way," the woman said.

"You have sharp ears," Joshua said. "One of them . . . and another discipline."

"I once became curious about things like that and studied enough so I could write a dance that would be realistic. Perhaps I should have paid more attention to the effects rather than merely the motions."

"And perhaps," Joshua said dryly, "I should have paid more attention to the end product of the motions myself."

"You mean you should not have intervened."

"I won't say that. But someone taking a quiet vacation doesn't need the sort of attention I most likely just set myself up for."

"Yes," the woman said. "A 'vacationer' mustn't ever get in the spotlight." She put obvious quotation marks around 'vacationer.' "When you are not on 'vacation,' might I ask how you spend your time?"

"Traveling. Meeting people."

"That covers quite a range of professions," the woman said.

"It does, doesn't it?" Joshua agreed. "By the way, we haven't formally met." He introduced himself.

"I am Candia Hsui," the woman said. "One-half of the Null-G Duo. I'm afraid, the way I feel at present, I may be all of the troupe. Damn Megaris, anyway!"

"Your partner?"

"At the moment. What a shit! You have no idea, Joshua, what it is like to look for a dance partner. I don't care that they're always boy-crazy or that they have the courage of bush babies.

"What I just said is a lie, but I try to be content with what Allah wills. None of them seems to think they have to be strong. I've spent more time in clinics getting patched up because some wavy boy dropped me than anything else." Joshua realized she was babbling, a little shocky from the blow and the blood.

"Shows what happens," he said, trying a mild joke, "when you take your job home with you. You should've left him at the office."

Candia giggled suddenly. "You have humor in you," she said. "That is good. That is better than Elois or most of the men I generally choose."

"Elois is—was, rather—your companion by law?"

"Choice only. I would never contract with anyone. Love does not live as long as lawyers."

"You have humor, too," Joshua said.

"I think you must," Candia said, "especially when you are as long from home as I am. Here. This is my lifter."

It was a sleek black-silver sporter. She touched the lock, and the bubble opened.

"Let me ask you something," Joshua said. "Where are you going?"

"Why—" Candia broke off. "I was going to say back to my apartments. Which I share—shared with Elois. I do not think I am thinking clearly.

"Hell! What a pain that will be. I'll have to get my cases tomorrow and no doubt have to put up with another session from the bastard. Although he never struck me but once before."

"If you want to pick them up now, I'll ride along," Joshua said, wondering why his tongue was behaving so foolishly. "I'll help you get a room at whatever hotel you choose. If you're short on a payday . . ." He let the suggestion trail into silence.

"No. Money is not something I am short of, but rather common sense. Get in. Let us go, get my things, and be gone before Elois finishes getting his arm sewn up or plassed or whatever they'll do to him."

Joshua went to the other side of the lifter and clambered in. Candia touched buttons, and the bubble closed, the drive started, and the vehicle lifted off the ground.

The lifter went through the resort streets swiftly, past the still-raucous bars and restaurants, then into the hills, past the dark, blank-faced palaces of Trinité's elite. She drove the winding roads fast, skillfully.

"What was it you did to Elois? I thought I saw a knife, but it was black."

"It was a knife. Of sorts. I'm sorry I had to use it. Usually there's an easier way."

"Pah! I hope the pigfutterer bleeds to death!"

Elois's "apartments" were a rather luxurious town house atop one of Morne-des-Esses's peaks.

Wolfe looked at it. "Quite a place. What does Elois do to pay for it?"

"Some of this, some of that. Mostly smuggle. Nothing seamy, he swore. Just papers that are worth money on other worlds that people wish to have in other places without handling them themselves. I should have known what he was, seeing his bullies always about him." She shrugged. "At least he was fun for a while."

Candia touched the lock, swore when nothing happened. "He already took my porepattern from the lock! Now I will have to come back and listen to his bullshit!"

"Maybe not."

Joshua touched the tips of his fingers to the sides of the lock and *listened*. The lock clicked, and the door swung open. Candia looked at him in astonishment.

"How did you do that? Elois said this lock was unbreakable! In his trade having a safe place is very important."

"Perhaps he should complain to the manufacturer," Joshua suggested.

Candia's possessions were indeed no more than three cases. Joshua lifted the last of them into the baggage area of the lifter, slammed the lid closed, and got in the vehicle.

Candia climbed into the driver's seat. "Now, what hotel would you recommend, my fearless paladin?"

"One with two big doormen," Joshua suggested.

"Elois looks like the type who doesn't take no for an easy answer."

"Probably not," the woman sighed. "In which event I shall have the law take him by the balls and pull hard. Let me think. Perhaps the Diamant Novotel?" She looked at him in a curious manner.

"You know Diamant better than I do," Wolfe said. "I've only been onplanet a day."

"We'll go there," Candia said, giving him the strange look once more.

There were two doormen at the Novotel even at that late hour, and both of them were very large. They hurried out as the lifter slipped up the drive.

"There is an advantage to an expensive toy like this," Candia said. "People scrape and bow when they see you come. I could be an ax murderer and no one would notice." She sighed. "What a bother it will be giving it back to Elois."

The bubble opened, and the two men bowed Candia and Joshua out, then picked up her luggage.

"I'll wait until you sign in," he said, "then let you sort things out in peace."

"You know," she murmured, "I am starting to believe you might truly be *sans peur et sans reproche*."

"Don't put big money on that," Joshua said. "Unless you change *reproche* to *raison*. But thanks for the compliment. Why?"

The doormen withdrew discreetly out of hearing.

"You never suggested that a good place to stay might be your hotel and the safest place of all would be your room and your bed. I've not known many men who wouldn't try to take such advantage."

"But I'm not staying in a hotel."

"Your villa, then."

"Nor there."

Candia glared at him. "I do not know whether to stamp my foot, hit you, or laugh. Very well, then, Joshua Wolfe. Where are you staying?

"My ship's moored in the harbor. The *Grayle*."

"Thank you, Joshua. Perhaps your chivalry will be rewarded. We shall see." She came close, stood on tiptoe, kissed Wolfe on the lips, and went into the hotel without looking back.

Joshua stood, bemused, still feeling that butterfly touch. He realized one of the doormen was grinning at him.

Wolfe licked his lips, tasted something like jasmine, and went down the hill to the harbor.

* CHAPTER ELEVEN *

There were two scribed messages on the com when
Joshua awoke:

*I would appreciate a few moments of your time at
ten in the morning, in my office, if it would be convenient, so that we can both avoid possible problems.*
                                        Falster Samothrake
                                        General Manager
                                        Casino d'Or

and:

*Perhaps my hero would wish a bit of a reward this after-
noon. If so, please have an appetite and be waiting at one in the
afternoon.*

                                                    Candia

Joshua looked at them and grimaced. "So the tiger

gets his innings first." He yawned and went to the workout room.

Falster Samothrake was the bullet-headed man Joshua had taken for a security thug.

"Mister Wolfe," he said in a flat voice, expressionless. "Please sit down."

Joshua obeyed. "I suppose I owe you an apology," he said.

"No. I've never minded being thought stupid. You should know what an excellent tool that becomes."

"I've been told that."

"You made quite a stir in my casino last night," Samothrake said.

"I didn't figure that you'd want one of your performers messed up."

"We have security for problems like that."

"I didn't see any around. So I did what I thought was necessary."

"Wouldn't you say you might have been a little excessive? There are three men in the hospital this morning. One will need extensive plastic surgery before he'll be happy looking at his face in the morning, the second has a shattered humerus, and the third will probably lose about thirty percent of the use of his hand."

"They brought the guns to the party," Joshua said. "What do you propose to do about what happened?"

"I wasn't sure, which was why I asked you to come here. I decided if you failed to show up, then my course of action would be clear. But you did.

"Mister Wolfe, I now plan to do exactly nothing. Let

me explain, so you may choose to regulate your actions here on Trinité accordingly.

"First is I watched your baccarat dealings yesterday. Very professional, sir. I like having a freelance such as yourself at my tables. It encourages others to play against you, since all wish to tear down the master, and every time the fools bet, the house takes its percentage.

"Second is that I'm familiar with Mister Elois. He is, to put it bluntly, an arrogant pain in the ass. He's been a problem here before. Perhaps, when and if his hand heals, he will moderate his behavior, although I doubt it.

"Third is I intensely disliked his involvement with Miss Hsui. I would never dream of intervening in one of our performers' personal lives, but I am most content when *they* are and I knew that to be unlikely with any-one who chooses to company Mister Elois.

"The fourth reason is the most significant, however. You have important friends."

Joshua raised an eyebrow.

"I refer to the Hofeis. They were happy to tell me just what happened outside the casino last night and wished to make certain I didn't get any incorrect ideas. Since they are the principal owners of Thule Invest-ments, which owns twelve points in this casino, I was, of course, most interested in what they had to say."

"The Hofeis?" Joshua was incredulous.

"Indeed. They prefer to travel without fanfare, and their tastes tend toward the commonplace. Perhaps that is why Thule Investments is so successful. I truly be-lieve the Hofeis could almost buy this world if they wished.

"You still appear astonished at who your friends turned out to be, which is another clue I chose the right course to take, since I loathe a gold digger."

"Thanks," Joshua said. "But what about the Diamant police?"

"They see and know what certain people in this city, of which I am one, wish them to. No more, no less.

"One other, minor point. You asked me about some-one named Edet Sutro. Might I inquire as to your interest? I must add that if you're planning anything with him such as occurred last night, you will be in serious jeopardy. Mister Sutro is one of the most honored citizens of Diamant and a valued patron of this establishment."

"Not at all," Wolfe reassured him. "Before I decided to visit Trinité, I discussed matters with some of my colleagues, particularly as to men they knew on this world who might be fond of some exclusive action. He was but one of the names given me."

"Exclusive action." Samothrake mused. "That would mean, to a man in your evident profession, someone who likes a high-stakes game and isn't that quick at calculating the odds."

Wolfe inclined his head, said nothing.

"I'll give you this, Mister Wolfe. Your friends advised you poorly. Mister Sutro is quite a capable sportsman. I can attest to that by personal experience."

"Thank you for the information. While not questioning your word, I'm well aware each shepherd prefers to have his own flock to shear."

The two men exchanged wintery smiles.

"Feel free to test the truth of what I said when Mister

Sutro returns to Trinité." Samothrake rose. "Now, I'm afraid I have problems more complicated than yours. Thank you for coming to see me, Mister Wolfe. Please feel free to continue using our facilities, although I will caution you that the next set of unusual events may be seen in a less forgiving light."

The *Dolphin* cut its drive, and Thetis tossed a line around a mooring cleat on the *Grayle*'s loading platform. Her only passenger was Candia, who wore a translucent wrap of swirling colors, sandals, and a beach hat. It was exactly one.

"Good afternoon, my brave knight," she said. "You look rested."

"Candia. Thetis."

The girl's greeting was a bit clipped, and she turned away, busying herself with a rag on the instrument panel's brasswork.

"Shall we be on our way?" Candia asked. "I have all that could be desired by the hungriest dragon slayer." She indicated a large cooler behind her seat.

"I didn't know what you'd planned," Joshua said. "Am I dressed appropriately?"

Candia eyed his sleeveless cotton vest, shorts, and ankle-strapped sandals.

"You are perfect. Now get in."

The *Dolphin* nosed into the beach and grounded with a slight scrape. Joshua leapt over the side. The water was cool, perfectly clear. Candia struggled with the heavy cooler, and Joshua took it from her, waded to the islet's beach, and came back to help her out of the boat. Candia had a small mesh bag in her hand.

"I'll be back when you told me to, Miss Hsui," Thetis said. "I hope you two have fun."

Without waiting for a response, she moved controls, and water frothed as the *Dolphin* backed off the beach, turned, and headed back toward Morne-des-Esses.

"That one does not like me," Candia said.

"Why not?"

"Because she sees me as a rival."

Joshua blinked. "But she's just a kid."

"I know some men who would think that an attraction," Candia said. "And what if she is? When you were young, didn't you ever wildly love someone who did not know you even breathed?"

Joshua's face softened. "Yes," he remembered. "She was nineteen. I was sixteen. She was the daughter of the Federation secretary of state."

"What happened?"

"Nothing. I was trying to get courage enough to ask her to my academy's formal ball. Of course she would have laughed. She was a very cool one with an eye for the main chance, and my parents were vastly outranked by those of the boys who usually came calling. But I was lucky, and my father was transferred to a new post, off Earth, so my heart was only chipped a little bit around the edges."

"So you have been on Earth?" Candia's eyes were wide.

"Born there. Grew up all over the galaxy. My parents were career diplomats."

"How interesting. I shall be interested in hearing

your stories and seeing if perhaps we have visited the same worlds.

"Now, come." She took a small clock from her bag and put it on the top of the cooler. "There is much to be done before the young one returns to make sure I have not stolen your virginity.

"First a swim. That is good for the appetite."

Candia stripped off the robe. She wore a black fishnet one-piece suit that had a silver-looking fastener strip down the front. She ran to the edge of the water. "But I hate the feel of clothes when I am swimming," she called back. Her fingers opened the fastener, and she pulled the suit down to her thighs, side kicked it off, caught it with one hand, and tossed it back at Joshua.

"You have my permission to be equally immodest," she shouted. She ran three steps into the water, flat dove, and vanished.

Joshua shook his head, smiling, then took off his clothes and went after her.

The world was calm, blue, at peace. A small fish looked skeptically at Joshua; its tail wriggled, and then it was gone. Joshua kicked toward a brightly striped mass of seaweed growing from the sea bottom. It was shallow off this nameless island, no more than fifteen feet deep.

He'd looked for Candia but hadn't found her, above or below the surface, and so swam happily about, with Trinité, Al'ar, violence all of another world and time.

Something tickled his toes, and he jackknifed and was face to face with Candia. She stuck her tongue out and swam for the surface.

Joshua broke water a second after she did.

"You are careless," she chided. "What if I were a man-eating fish?"

"Then I would have been doomed, and you would have had to eat the whole lunch yourself."

"What a tragedy," she said, and swam close to him, floating effortlessly. She put her arms around him.

"It could be I *am* a man-eater. Be warned." She giggled. "I was watching you swim. You are very graceful."

"Thank you."

Her eyes closed, and her lips opened. Joshua kissed her.

"Perhaps the reason you swim so well," she said, "is the excellence of your rudder."

She brought her legs up around his thighs and pulled him close against her. Joshua felt his stiffness against her warmth. He thrust gently, experimentally.

"Ah ah," Candia said. "If I let you do that, you will not be able to steer yourself and will never navigate back to our lunch." She broke out of the embrace, eeled backward, and swam hard for the beach.

"I would say we did very well," Candia said, surveying the ruins. "The artichoke hearts and olives are gone, as is the caviar. The cheeses have been destroyed. There's a bit of the pâté left if you have not made a sufficient pig of yourself."

"I'm so full, I'll never move," Joshua said.

"Ah? Not even for some more champagne?"

"For that I can move." Joshua lazily extended his glass.

Candia picked up the bottle and leaned back on the picnic cloth. She wore only the rainbow robe.

"Perhaps m'sieu would wish a new glass," she murmured. She opened her robe and let a bit of champagne trickle into her navel.

"M'sieu wishes," Joshua said, a bit hoarse, and slid over to her. His lips caressed her stomach, moved up, his hands slipping the robe aside, and his teeth teased the nipples of her tiny breasts. Then he moved downward, and Candia opened the robe for him and spread her legs.

His tongue fondled, entered her, and she gasped and lifted her legs around his shoulders.

"Next," she managed, "it will be my turn for dessert."

"I feel," Joshua said, watching the *Dolphin* approach the beach, "like I'm coming home from an evening out and my mother's about to decide if I was a good boy or not."

"Don't worry about her." Candia laughed. "Of course she knows."

"How could she?"

"She is a woman, is she not?"

Thetis looked at them both, her lips pursed angrily, and had even less to say on the ride back to the *Grayle*.

"It doesn't feel like a woman has ever lived here," Candia announced after Wolfe had shown her around the ship.

"No. Not for long. But how did you know?"

"It is comfortable but stiff. A man's place. But that is good. Are you coming to see me dance tonight?"

"I hope so. Are you now a solo act?"

"No. I gave Megaris another chance. I am always doing that, I fear."

"Afterward, do you want to come back here?"

"Of course."

"You know, if you wish, you could bring your luggage with you."

Candia looked surprised. "I know I am quite good in bed, but this is quite sudden." A cunning look crossed her face. "Ah, but perhaps I think too much of myself. Tell me the truth, Joshua Wolfe. I know you are not on vacation here, nor do I believe you are a gambler.

"The men I have known who were could never absent themselves from the tables for long, nor did they have the ability to relax and enjoy a simple picnic and swim.

"Could I be right in thinking that my presence here, with you, might help you do whatever you are on Trinité for?"

Joshua hesitated, then remembered what he'd told Lil back on Platte. "You're right, Candia. And yes, you could help."

"Will it be dangerous?" Without waiting for a reply: "I hope so. I have been living such a dull life of late. That was another complaint I had about Elois. He kept me well clear of his business. All I was good for was as a bed partner, that for not very long, then someone to get angry with and finally strike.

"So excite me, Joshua. I shall try to do my share in return."

* * *

Joshua had just finished dressing to go out when the ship told him the *Dolphin* was pulling up at the platform. He'd eaten on the ship after Candia had left, not wishing to test his digestion against the casino's efforts again.

Thetis was the only one aboard. She had a large plastic envelope under her arm. Wolfe hesitated, then invited her inside.

"I'm a butt," she said.

"Nice opening. Why?"

"Oh ... I was rude this afternoon. I wasn't professional. I'm sorry. I thought—anyway, I didn't have any right."

Wolfe started to say something, remembered sleepless nights and the Federation official's daughter, and changed his mind. "Forget it. Everybody's entitled to a mood every now and then."

Thetis brightened. "That's good. Thanks. I won't do it again. The main reason I had to come out was I've found your Mister Sutro! And I know an awful lot about him!"

She beamed, and Joshua grinned.

"Sit down," she ordered, and touched the fastener on the envelope and took out papers. "Now the Sibyl of Cumae will hold forth. Knows all, sees all, and will talk your ear off about it.

"Sutro. First name, Edet. Naturalized citizen of Trinité for about ten years, since right after the war. No police record. Nobody knows where he came from before that. Grampa got that," she explained, "from a fishcop he used to be friends with who doesn't know things are different now.

"I'll get a picture of Sutro tomorrow. He's big, people said, and has a beard.

"He calls himself an expediter, which Grampa said can mean almost anything. He owns an island he's named Thrinacia. I had to look that up—"

"I know what it was. He has a nasty choice of names."

"I think he's probably nasty in other ways," Thetis said. "Anyway, Thrinacia is one of the Outer Islands, about forty miles off Morne-des-Esses. I've been out to the islands three or four times. We could get to Thrinacia with the *Dolphin* on a calm day, or you could rent a lifter. I looked it up on the chart, and it's about a mile long by two miles wide. It's got its own robot instrument-approach spaceport, two or three separate mansions, and a sheltered docking area. The island's surrounded on three sides with cliffs. They're not very high, no more than fifty feet, and I think you could climb them if you wanted. The other side, the one with the dock, has some beaches."

"Let's go back to this cliff climbing for a minute," Joshua said. "What do you think I am?"

Thetis looked at him wisely, then back to her papers. "He has twelve men working for him. *I* found that out. Do you know how? I'm real proud of myself."

"Tell me."

"There's only about three groceries that cater to the people who live off Morne-des-Esses. Naturally, since I do a lot of the deliveries, I know all of them pretty well.

"Mister Sutro does his shopping at Sentry Markets,

and I found out from the manager there's an open charge account with thirteen authorized signatures. I double-checked, and there's twelve different kinds of liquor they keep on hand, so I figured that was a pretty good confirmation."

She grinned excitedly at Wolfe. "Wouldn't I make a great spy?"

"No," Wolfe said. "You're too pretty and not loony enough."

"That's what Granddad said. About not being crazy enough. Thank you.

"Mister Sutro has a big fishing boat, a speedster, and two lifters registered. One of them is a heavy grav-lighter; the other's a sporter. All of them are on the island.

"He's gone—offworld—about six months out of the year, maybe more. He's gone right now, by the way."

Joshua grimaced, said nothing.

"I thought you might be interested in when he leaves the island," Thetis went on, "so I talked to the harbormaster and checked the log.

"He generally comes ashore once a week or so when he's on Trinité. He always comes to Diamant within a day or two after he's come back from offplanet. Grandpa checked the logs against Diamant Subcontrol's history of landings. They clear all approaches for the islands as well as here. He never lands at Wule that I could find out.

"His men do the shopping and so forth, and they generally use the cargo lighter.

"When he comes in, he does the same thing. He brings a bunch of his guys with him. I found out they're pretty mean-looking people, like some of the rich folks here use for bodyguards."

"That's exactly what they'd be," Joshua put in.

"I asked some more questions, but people started giving me strange looks and I had to stop. But I found out that he likes to gamble, like you told me. Generally he gambles up at the Mushroom Tabernacle."

"The what?"

"That's what we call the main casino," she explained. "Sometimes he goes to the Palace—that's the second of the big gambling places—but not very often. I couldn't find out what kind of games he likes to play.

"I even went to one of the girl places," she said. "I asked about Mister Sutro, and the madam told me I was quote way the hell too young to be caring what Sutro does with his diddlestick and get the hell out of her front room, so I struck out there."

"Thetis, you *are* too young to be doing things like that," Joshua complained.

The girl stared at him. "Maybe you'd be surprised, Mister Wolfe." Then she turned pink and started stuffing the papers back into the envelope. "Anyway. That's all I've got."

Wolfe got up, went to his cache, and took out bills. Then he remembered something, went up from the living area into his trip cabin, and fumbled through drawers. He found a long case that held something he'd meant to give a woman who'd turned out not to be what he'd thought and went back to the main room.

"Here."

He gave her the sheaf of credits.

"Hell!" she gasped. "That's too much money!"

"No, it's not. You earned it, plus it comes out of expenses. Your grandfather gets half. I'll be needing him for some night work if he's available." He gave the case to Thetis. She looked at it, then at him suspiciously, and opened it.

Inside, on a red plush nest, was a torque bracelet made of precious metals twined together until the ornament gleamed with a dozen different colors, though each appeared to blend seamlessly with the others.

"My. My, oh, my," she managed in a whisper.

"That's your tip."

She picked up the bracelet, slipped her hand through it, and examined it. Then she lifted her eyes.

"Thank you, Joshua. Thank you."

He put on his formal jacket, tucked a small gun into its hidden holster, went to the casino, played half a dozen abstracted hands, and deservedly lost all of them.

He saw the Hofeis as they came in for dinner and thanked them enormously.

"Forget it," Arabo said briefly. "Nobody should ever put hands on a woman."

"And it was so *exciting*," Dorena added. "Although I never dreamed a real fight was that bloody.

"If you want to pay us back, you can make good on your promise to teach us a little about gambling."

Wolfe grinned. "I have a question. Why would two people who don't know anything about gambling buy part of a casino?"

Arabo looked puzzled. "I don't see what that has to do with it. I know people like to make love, so if I wanted to buy a whorehouse, would I have to be a customer?"

"You'd better not," Dorena warned. "Or you'd be wearing your knockers for a necklace."

"I know people like to gamble," Arabo went on, ignoring his wife, "especially rich people. There aren't a lot of places in this sector of the Outlaw Worlds where it's safe, and the Casino d'Or had the best balance sheet, a good reputation with the Diamant police, and their employees seem to stay on, which is always the sign of a good company.

"What else did I need to know?"

Joshua decided he would never be able to fathom the mind of a businessperson and left them.

He sat through the show, including Candia's dancing, without much registering. He was thinking about a large bearded man, twelve bodyguards, and an island.

* CHAPTER TWELVE *

Candia moaned, leaned back, hands on Joshua's knees, then leaned forward again and again as Joshua's hand caressed her. Her body jolted, her head went back in a silent scream, then she sagged forward onto his chest, gasping for air. Her breathing slowed after a time.

"You are still ready," she said in some surprise.

"Next time I'll finish, too."

"Does your Way teach that kind of control?"

"Yes."

"Why is it not more popular?"

Joshua was silent for a space, then decided to tell her the truth. "Because, for one thing, it helps to have been a prisoner of the Al'ar for three years."

Candia was jolted. "Oh. I did not know. Joshua, I am sorry. Now you are soft. Please. Forget I spoke. Think of something else. Think of loving me as you did a moment ago. As you will again. As I want you."

Joshua breathed, measured, bringing control. *Water,*

144

flow . . . water, move . . . water, change, and his body responded.

"Now," she whispered. "Now we shall do it my way."

Without freeing him, she pushed herself up and lifted a leg across his chest.

"Turn sideways," she said, "until your feet hang off the edge of the bed." Joshua obeyed. She swiveled once more until her legs were on the outside of his.

"Ah, I feel you. Now, sit up. Slowly. Yes. Now I shall do all the moving. You can use your hands as you wish on me." She moved her hips up, down, a steady motion.

"You know," she said, voice throaty, "I think all dancers dream of having . . . another dancer for their lover. Someone who has the muscles they do, someone who can move with them. Why we do not think of a fighter, a lover . . . Oh. Yes. Touch me there more. But . . . it seems men dancers always choose each other. Oh! Like that, Joshua. Oh, yes. But now I know the place to look. Ah now. Now I am coming. Come with me. I want to feel you let go!"

Her body pulsed around him, and he jerked upward, stifling his outcry.

"You said your ship talks to you."

"Yes."

"It sees what's going on outside?"

"It does."

"Inside, too?"

"Yes."

"So it knows what we are doing?"

"I don't know if it can interpret what it sees. Perhaps it can. Does it matter?"

"I don't know. But I have never been watched by a machine before. I don't know if I find it exciting . . . or creepy."

Joshua threw another bucket of cold water on the stones, and steam swirled through the small room.

"That is all," Candia gasped. "I have suffered enough for my sins! Let me out. I'm boiled!"

She pulled the sauna door open and staggered out, and Joshua heard her splash into the pool before the door swung to.

Two bucketfuls later he, too, stumbled out into the chilled air of the bathroom. Candia lay in the small pool, her splayed legs on its rim, head pillowed on an inflatable cushion. Water bubbled around her.

"I tried to talk to your ship," she said, "but it ignores me."

"It *can't* acknowledge you. That's in its basic programming."

"It's probably jealous." She sighed. "But that's all right. You have a very sexy ship, you know."

"No, I didn't know."

"Look. As soon as I got in here, pumps started up. I could just lie here like this, letting myself be loved by the water, and sooner or later forget about men."

"Candia, you are oversexed."

"I would certainly hope so," the woman murmured. "I want to be able to keep up with you."

"Enough fooling about," Joshua said. "We've got to be out and about."

Reluctantly the dancer came out of the pool. "So what are we going to do?"

"We're renting a nice, comfortable house on our own island. I've decided I need more privacy. A house and a lifter, and I'd like to put them in your name."

Joshua stayed in the background while the sleek, dapper little man danced attendance on his client. Candia looked at Wolfe when a question came that she couldn't answer, and he'd nod—slightly.

It took only four islands before they had what he needed. The island had a single house, a sprawling, fully roboticized villa, so there wouldn't be any nosy staff. There was a boathouse and a dock. The nearest occupied island was three miles away.

It was about ten miles off Morne-des-Esses, far enough to be able to lose any pursuit.

The realtor beamed when Candia gave her approval. He went to fetch the lease papers from his lifter.

"Tell me," she whispered, "why you chose this one. Was it the mirrors on the bedroom ceiling? Or the size of that big bed?"

"Neither," Joshua said. "It was the goat I saw out back."

"Pervert!"

The ship hovered up to the dock, and the lock slid open. Joshua set two travel cases on the dock, then stepped out.

The lock closed. Joshua touched his bonemike, spoke inaudibly, and the ship turned, went out about fifty meters, and disappeared beneath the water.

"That is eerie," Candia decided. "What happens if she decides not to come up again when you call her?"

"Then I've got a very expensive salvage problem."

"The water is very clear. Someone might be able to look down and see her, you know."

"If anybody's looking straight down for a spaceship, my cover's blown, anyway. All we can do is hope and think clean thoughts."

Candia picked up one case with the dancer's strength that Joshua was still surprised at, and they started toward the house.

"Now what do we do? Besides make love, I mean."

"Mostly, we wait."

"So what'll you want with me? I'll guess it ain't real legal or you'd have Thetis do it."

"Nothing illegal about it, Mister Libanos. Let's just say it's a bit chancy."

"Whyn't you use that fancy lifter you've got?"

"Lifters send up spray. I want something quiet."

"Why not?" the old man grunted. "Nothing much happening this time of year, anyway."

"Can I ask you something, Joshua?"

"You can *ask* anything."

"But you might not answer. It is a personal question. Very personal. You were a prisoner of the Al'ar, you said the first night we made love."

"I was." Joshua's voice was suddenly dead.

"I wish the light was on. I would like to see your face, to know when I should shut up."

"Don't worry about it. What's your question?"

"Were you a soldier?"

"Not then," Joshua said reluctantly. "When the war started . . . when the Al'ar attacked the Federation, I was on Sauros. That's one of the Al'ar Ruling Worlds, as they called them. They didn't have to centralize their capital, since they had ways of communicating between stars almost instantly. We still don't know how they did that.

"My family had been sent there two, almost three years before, when the first incidents occurred and things started heating up. They were supposed to try to defuse the situation with words.

"But after a while the Al'ar decided they didn't want to listen. I guess there weren't many on our side who wanted to, either, by then.

"When they blindsided our fleets without bothering to declare war, they rounded up every Federation being on any of their worlds. They didn't bother with the difference between soldiers and civilians. Not then, not later. I ended up in a camp."

"What about your parents?"

"They died, like most of the people around me. Disease. Malnutrition. Neglect. The Al'ar weren't deliberate bastards, but it worked out the same."

"But you escaped."

"I escaped."

"And after that?"

"I was the first human who'd been that close to them for that long, and so the Federation was very glad to see me and use what I knew. Later on there were a few more like me. But not very many. The Al'ar didn't take many prisoners, since they never surrendered themselves."

"Then the Federation made you a soldier?"

"Of sorts."

"I have known soldiers," Candia said softly, "and I have learned that none of them, none of the real ones, ever want to talk about fighting. So I shall not ask about what you did or where.

"But I have another question. How could you stand to be around those creatures? I never was; I only saw them on the vid or on holos. But they made me shudder. Like . . . like seeing a slug on your walk. Or a spider on your wall."

"That's the way most humans feel . . . felt. The Al'ar felt the same way about us. That's the real reason the war happened."

"But you didn't?"

"No."

"Why not?"

Wolfe was silent for a long time.

"I don't really know," he said slowly. "Maybe it's because spiders never bothered me. Or maybe because I got moved around so much growing up that I was always on the outside. Every place we went was new, and the people were strange. Most generally they didn't like me, because I was different."

"But they killed your parents. So you hated them and must hate them now."

"No," Joshua said. "No, I didn't. Not then, not now."

After two weeks no one much noticed Joshua around the casino. He was just another sleek gambler who happened to be Candia's latest lover.

He would take her to work and back to the island

most nights, generally spending the time in between at the table, where he usually won. Always courteous, always reticent, he kept himself to himself and became invisible in that world of flashy transients.

One night he pulled the lifter close to the employee entrance and escorted Candia inside. He'd timed his appearance close to showtime, so the ramp to the backstage entrance was deserted.

He went back to the lifter, took out a black satchel, and reentered the casino. The corridor was still empty. He went down it to an unmarked door and opened it. He'd picked the lock earlier in the day.

He closed the door behind him and used a jamb lock to secure it. The stairwell was gray and smelled of moisture, concrete, neglect.

He opened his satchel, took out coveralls that were marked CASINO STAFF with a name tag of KYRIA, and pulled them on. The only other thing the satchel contained was a gray metal box. It was stenciled: RELAY BOARD. DO NOT OPEN WITHOUT PROPER PRECAUTIONS. He touched the paint, made certain it was dry.

He went up two flights of stairs, opened the landing door, and came out in another corridor. He went past five interior doors, paused at the sixth. His hands blurred around the lock, and he heard a click.

He opened the door and looked out on the catwalks that spidered above the main theater. There were the lights, pulleys, lifts, flats, and ropes remotely operated by the production crew backstage, a level below. He found the open section of wall he'd chosen, turned four studs on the back of the metal box, and held it against the wall.

It held firm when he released it. He went out, relocked the door, and went on down to the main level. He stripped off the coveralls, then opened the door a crack. The corridor was vacant.

He left the building, drove to the main entrance, and entered, this time politely greeting three or four people he knew, pausing long enough to ask one of them the time, frowning, and pretending to reset his watch.

"Wake up! Joshua, wake up!"

"What is it?"

"You were dreaming. Not a good dream," Candia said. "I heard you grunt. You're sweating. And you were speaking a language I do not know. It gave me the shudders."

"Something like this?" He spoke a few words in Al'ar.

"Yes. That is it." She turned on the light, got up, went into the bathroom, came back with a towel, then began drying him gently.

"Do you want to tell me what the dream was?"

"I was dreaming about Sauros," Wolfe said slowly.

"What were you doing?"

"I was with my Al'ar friend, Taen. I guess he was my friend. I never asked him, and he never told me."

"What were you doing?"

"He was showing me places on the body where, if you just touch them, the person must die."

Candia shuddered. "No wonder you were grunting. What a terrible thing to dream!"

"No," Joshua said. "I was fascinated. Taen was help-

ing me translate those places on an Al'ar body to the
same spots on a man."

"This was a friend?" Candia's voice was incredulous.

"A friend. A teacher."

"Did he teach you anything other than ways to kill
people?"

Joshua started to answer, stopped. His words had
gone on too long. "Yes. But nothing worth talking
about."

"I do not believe you," Candia said after a pause.
"But each of us must have secrets. There. Now you are
dry. Think happy thoughts." She kissed him, turned off
the light, rolled away from him, and pretended to go to
sleep.

Joshua lay awake for a time. Thinking. Remembering:

"Very well," Taen said. "I have decided I am mad.
I shall teach you how to fight. But it will be necessary for you to learn more of our ways. A virai cannot fly unless it studies the winds."

The boy bowed.

"You will not like me as I teach," the Al'ar warned.
"I did not—perhaps do not—like the one who taught
me. But this is as it should be."

Without warning, his grasping organ came out at
stomach level, struck the boy, and sent him stumbling
down. Joshua hit hard, rolled sideways, tucked his feet
under himself, and was back up.

The Al'ar moved closer. Joshua snapped a kick;
Taen's grasping organ touched it, and Wolfe lost his
balance and fell heavily.

Once more, without outcry, he got up.

"Good," the Al'ar said approvingly. "Showing pain like a hatchling means your shell, your body, is not learning. But this is the last I shall praise you."

Another time:

"I know the ways of being invisible," the boy complained. "They're of another Way, but I've studied them."

"Tell me, wormling, of thy brilliance."

Joshua took a breath.

"You're not really invisible. You just move beyond someone's perception. To the side, above, below. Or else you use misdirection. Touch them on one shoulder, duck under when they turn, and they'll think they've observed the area.

"Another way is to use light, darkness. Move toward the greater light, the greater darkness, and you'll remain unseen."

"I shit on such mummeries," Taen said. "This is the Al'ar way." He moved to one side, then back, and Joshua's eyes hurt. He looked away, then back. Behind Taen was a table, and on it was a vase.

Now he could see the vase clearly.

The air shimmered, and the Al'ar returned.

"That is what I mean. It is harder when someone is looking directly at you, easier when their focus is set elsewhere and then they turn to you. But this is another thing you shall learn."

Joshua smiled in the darkness.

The Al'ar shuffled toward him, moving in a semicircle. Joshua turned, kept his face toward Taen, moved sideways. The Al'ar's grasping organ swept out, and Joshua ducked under it, tapped the organ with three knuckles, and *felt* Taen's pain. The Al'ar's leg lashed, and Joshua kicked it away.

Taen tottered, and Joshua snapped a frontal kick into his midsection, sending the lean alien sprawling. Taen curled his legs under himself for the rebound, saw Joshua standing above him, fist ready for the killing knuckle stroke, and let himself down.

"You have learned all I have. Now it is time for us to go out and seek a name for you. You must then study, but with other teachers. I must consult our Elders and study our codex for permission, but I feel it is time. When—if they agree, we shall go beyond Sauros, out into the dry lands, at night.

"Someone shall be waiting for us. I shall teach you the words you must use to him. You must study them so you make no mistakes and cause me to look like a blind one."

A final memory came to Joshua.

He was twenty. He was alone by the green haze that marked the limits of the prison camp. Cross into the haze and you died.

He paid the haze no mind. After almost three years it had become a part of him, as much a part as the long shabby huts, the constant hunger, the torn clothes, and the cold.

And the searing loneliness.

He did not allow himself to think of that.

Instead, he began his movements, as he did every day at dawn and dusk. Slowly, letting his mind be taken away.

"Hey! You!"

The peace left him. He turned.

There were four of them. One was the son of a man who'd been one of the embassy's lifter drivers before the war, before internment, and was his age. The second was one of the Marine guards who preferred being with younger men instead of the few survivors of his detachment. The other two he did not know other than that they were always seen with the driver's son.

All of them were heavier than Wolfe and had found ways to acquire more food than the allocated rations.

Wolfe did not respond.

They formed a semicircle around him, keeping about eight feet from him.

"We wanted to set you straight," the driver's son said. "Teach you we all gotta hang together an' remember we're men, not friggin' slugs. We ain't gonna be here forever, an' we'll need t' be ready when th' time comes to fight back.

"It ain't right, you doin' all this Al'ar shit. Tryin' to be like one a them. We been watchin', seein' you study them. Prob'ly wishin—"

Joshua was suddenly next to him, less than a foot away. Two fingers touched the young man's skull just at the angle of his jaw. He screamed in mortal agony and stumbled back.

The Marine was coming into some sort of a fighting stance, but before his hands came level with the ground, Joshua struck him with a backhand and he fell, trying to breathe, eyes popping.

The third and fourth were backing away, hands lifted.

"Pick up these other two," Wolfe said. "And do not ever come to me again. Do not speak to me, do not think of me.

"Am I understood?"

He did not wait for a response but turned his back. Once more he began the slow movements, facing the green haze, letting his mind study it, reach toward it, through it, beyond it.

He barely noted the scraping sound as they dragged the two men away.

The memories faded. Wolfe put his head down and slept.

"They're pretty alert, aren't they, even when the boss ain't around?" Libanos said, lowering the night glasses. "I count three. Two walking in the open, number three hangin' back waiting to see what happens."

"Four," Wolfe corrected. "There's another one about twenty yards in front, keeping just off the walkway. He's still . . . now he's moving again."

"Mister, you ain't even used the binocs. How'd you know that?"

"Good eyes. I lead a clean life."

The old man snorted and continued examining Edet Sutro's island. The *Dolpin* sat, drive idling silently, about two hundred meters offshore, tossing in the surf.

"All right. I've got their cargo lighter. Pretty standard. I make it as a Solar 500. Been on 'em. Run 'em. They're power pigs but fast. Maneuverable enough to get by. One man can run 'em; takes two if you're on instruments. Hell if I know what the inside'd be like. Anything from bare cargo space to yacht city." He handed the binocs to Wolfe, who examined the lifter.

"What about visibility?"

"Normal electronics, night amplification with helmets, maybe screens. Normal vision'd be the windscreen, the four ports on either side, and there's a screen in the overhead rigged to a pickup in the stern."

"Entrances?"

"Two hatches on either side of the driving compartment, one roof hatch, a big hatch for cargo on port and sta'board.

"Oh, yeah, there's two emergency exits. One right in the stern, high up, the other in the bottom of the hull, in case the thing flips."

"Very good." Wolfe mused. "I like something with a lot of doors." He fixed the craft in his mind, then handed the glasses back. "Shall we go, Mister Libanos? It's getting past my bedtime."

Candia shuddered and gasped as Wolfe drove inside her, then lifted her leg up, curling it around him, heel at the back of his neck, bringing her hips up against him.

A moment later she did the same with her other leg, linking her ankles, pulling hard as Wolfe convulsed and spasmed. Moments later she followed him, and her legs sagged down.

They returned together, hands moving on each other's sweat-slick bodies.

After a time she murmured, "You know, Joshua, sometimes I almost think I'm . . ." Her voice trailed off.

"Yes?"

Candia sighed. "Never mind. I almost said something that would have embarrassed us both."

* * *

"So that's what should happen," Wolfe finished. "When I'm finished, I'll be gone. What kind of back door will you three be needing?"

"Depends," Libanos said. "How many bodies'll be lyin' around for the heat to notice?"

"None, I hope."

"It don't matter, really," Libanos said. "Me an' Thetis, we'll have half Morne-des-Esses swearin' we were singin' hymns with them. People don't realize there's a whole lot more folks on Trinité than th' rich an' putrid.

"We'll have no problems, Mister Wolfe."

"I didn't really think you would. Candia, what do you want to do? Since we've been seen being together, you'll most likely have to answer quite a few questions."

The dancer shrugged. "I, too, am not unfamiliar with fooling the law. But is that my only choice?"

"What would you rather do?"

Candia looked pointedly at Thetis and her grandfather. Libanos took the girl's arm, ignored her angry glare, and walked out onto the beach house's verandah.

"I'd rather go with you," the woman said, then held up a hand. "Wait. I didn't mean for it to sound like it did. I meant . . . you'll be leaving Trinité after you get whatever you want from this Sutro, am I correct?"

"Yes," Wolfe said.

"I would like a ride to wherever you're going, if I would not be in the way."

"What about your contract here?"

"Eh! It had only another month to run, and I am getting very bored of that horrible band's *crash-bang-boom* and being dropped by Megaris. I seek other pastures.

"And as you saw, I travel light." She looked away from Wolfe, out the window, the sunlight a white glare on her face.

"That would be good," Wolfe said. "It'd leave nothing but questions with nobody to answer them." He paused. "I'd feel a lot better, as well."

After a moment Candia turned and smiled at him.

They were on the beach. Candia had her head pillowed on his stomach. He was half-asleep, listening to her tell him about her early days in dance and how hard it had been to choose between ballet and what she did now.

"But eventually I thought perhaps I might like to live without constant pain and have a credit or two as well, and so—"

The com buzzed. Wolfe picked it up.

"Yes."

"I just heard on my scanner," Thetis's voice said. "Edet Sutro's ship has just been cleared to land on Thrinacia."

The sun and Candia and the dappled water vanished, and the darkness drew Wolfe in.

* CHAPTER THIRTEEN *

The man who'd named himself Edet Sutro grinned jovially as the lifter settled at the dock. "All right, boys, who plays and who stays?"

One of his bodyguards, whose expensive suit hung like it was still on a store rack, grimaced. "Me an' Pare lost th' roll."

"Look at it this way, Baines. You're saving your money keeping away from the tables."

"Right, boss. Thanks, boss. Three weeks on th' ship each way, plus sittin' in that damned jungle waitin' for a month, and now I'll get to wait till next time we come to town to spin down. I feel *lots* better. Thanks again."

The big man boomed laughter. "All right, boys. Let's go see what kind of mischief we can get into."

The smooth machine went into motion. Two men went up the companionway, doubled to the far side of the dock, looked over, saw nothing, then ran to each end of the pier, hands hovering inside their jackets. The second two went no farther than the top of the companionway and waited for Sutro to come up the ladder. They and the two behind the fence were as big as the bearded man.

If guns went off, it would be their duty to throw themselves on top of him and take the blast if they couldn't shoot first.

The last two came up onto the planking, ignored the others, and turned, scanning across the harbor.

Sutro strolled up the dock as if unaware that he wasn't alone.

"Man takes care," Libanos said. "You think we stand a chance?"

"That's what makes life interesting, isn't it?" Wolfe said. They appeared to be two idle strollers considering the rigging of a yacht that just happened to obscure the line of sight between them and the cargo lighter moored at the casino's dock a few dozen yards away.

"Mister Sutro," Samothrake said, voice as smooth as his slight bow, "it has been too long."

"It surely has, Falster," Sutro said. "It surely has."

"I trust your business offworld went well."

"My business almost always goes well," Sutro said. "I spend a great deal of time and care making sure."

Samothrake looked to either side and came closer. "There was a man asking about you."

"Ah?" Sutro beckoned his chief guard, Rosser, over.

Samothrake described Joshua Wolfe, named him. Sutro looked mildly interested, and Rosser's eyes vacuumed the casino. The other seven men pretended to pay attention to the hotel manager, but their eyes were always moving, always elsewhere, waiting.

"Is he here tonight?"

"No, sir. But I do expect him. He is friends with one of our dancers and generally arrives with her before the dinner show."

"I see. Perhaps when this Mister Wolfe shows up you'd do us both the honor of introductions."

"I would be delighted." Again Samothrake bowed, and Rosser, at Sutro's nod, unobtrusively passed him a bill.

"Now," Sutro said, his voice booming, several passersby turning to look. "What first? Drinks, then some action, eh?"

His bodyguards chorused enthusiasm, and the small throng moved toward one of the casino's lounges.

Candia stepped onto the dock.

"You'll be right here?" she asked skeptically.

"I'll be back here as soon as I make the call," Thetis said. "I promised Joshua. Nobody'll bother me."

She opened her windbreaker, and Candia saw she had a pistol stuck in her waistband. "Granddad gave me this and taught me to use it, to make sure I'm not bothered. There's been folks who thought they were buying more'n a runabout when they gave me money. They didn't think that way for very long.

"You just worry about being seen and establishing your alibi, like you're supposed to do. As soon as the excitement starts, you come running."

The girl and the woman exchanged looks of mutual

dislike, then applied smiles, and the dancer hurried toward the casino.

"Faites vas jeux, messieurs," the *tourneur* said, teeth flashing white under his thin mustache.

"Passe," Sutro said, and tossed credits onto that square. There was a gabble in various languages as other bettors chose their lots.

"I like a live game like this. I surely can't stand playing roulette with one of those goddamned robots," Sutro observed.

"Might as well play a vid game," Rosser said. The *tourneur* bobbed his head, indicating agreement as he twirled the wheel's cross-handles. At the same moment he spun the small ivory wheel against the wheel's turning.

The ball bounced, skipped, red, black, then red, slowing.

"Rien ne va plus," the *tourneur* announced unnecessarily—most of the numbers were filled. The ball bounced once more, then came to rest.

"Sept," the tourneur said. One croupier pulled in credits with his rake, and a second paid the winnings. Sutro watched his money depart, expression neutral. He held out a hand, and Rosser put another sheaf of bills in it.

"Mister Sutro?"

Sutro frowned at the interruption, turned. Samothrake stood beside him.

"The gentleman you wished to meet will not be in this evening," the casino manager said, attempting to sound as if the news were personally tragic. "I was advised by his friend that he is ill."

"Perhaps another time," Sutro said indifferently.

"Messieurs, faites vas jeux," the dapper little man said once more.

Sutro sipped champagne, considered the wheel.

"Dernière douzaine," he decided.

Thetis slipped thin gloves on, put a coin in the vid, touched sensors. She fitted a round filter over the vid's mike. As the screen swirled into life, she blanked her own pickup with a square of plas.

Wolfe stepped out of his coveralls and was wearing a skintight black plas suit. Libanos stood beside him, holding a very large, very antique projectile weapon.

"Put it away," Wolfe advised. "Nobody needs to see you waving that cannon around."

Libanos muttered, obeyed.

Wolfe took a dart gun from a small pack, clipped the gun to a catch on the suit, put the pack on, pulled the suit's hood over his head, and went down the ladder into the water.

He entered it without a splash and swam slowly, effortlessly, across the dark harbor, hands never coming above the water's surface. He swam to the rear of the lifter and then clung to the still-warm drive outlet.

Breathe in . . . deep, deep, diaphragm deep . . . out . . . in again . . .

His heart was a slow, steady metronome.

He reached out, *felt* the man lounging behind the controls of the ship, *breathe . . . breathe . . . found* the thin man at the port, eyes watching the dock.

A shadow came out of the water and pulled itself onto the narrow step at the lighter's stern. Wolfe eyed a pickup mounted above him, decided it wasn't turned on, and found the emergency hatch. It was latched shut on the inside. Wolfe pried at it, tore a nail, flinched. He took a thin-bladed knife from its sheath at his waist and gently probed between the hatch and the hull, eyes closed.

The blade met resistance, and Joshua pushed. The latch's *click* was crashingly loud, but only to him.

He looked behind, saw nothing in the harbor that would outline him, and lifted the hatch.

Baines grunted. "Your turn. My eyes are bleedin'." There was no response.

Baines turned away from the port, frowning, saw Pare's body slumped in the seat, and black blurred at him; a finger speared, touching his forehead, and the thin man folded to the deck.

Wolfe put plas ties on both men's hands and feet, took a red-shielded flash from his pack, and blinked it once, twice toward the wharf where Libanos was waiting.

"Calm down, Dorothy. What is it?"

"A bomb, Mister Samothrake! Somebody planted a bomb here!"

"Don't get excited. No matter what's going to happen, you won't make it any easier if you get hysterical. How do you know?"

"Someone just called. They wouldn't give me a picture. They said there was a bomb—bombs—and we were all going to die for our wickedness!"

Samothrake's voice remained calm. "You're new here. We get those kind of things all the time. They're either fruitbars or kids. What did the voice sound like?"

"I couldn't tell. It sounded synthed. Flat. Maybe a woman."

"What *exactly* did it say? Try to remember."

"I can remember." The woman shuddered. "I'll never forget it. 'Ye . . .' That's what the voice said—ye. '. . . are the spawn of evil, wallowing in your degeneracy. Ye have been called, and there is no escape. I have set bombs to destroy your works unutterably. There shall be one for a warning, then others to destroy everything.' That's exactly what was said. I was trained to remember things like that."

"That's why we hired you on the switchboard," Samothrake said.

"What do we do?"

Samothrake considered, looking at the thronged gaming floor.

The glowing hand swept across the top of Wolfe's watch, and his thumb touched a sensor.

The "relay box" exploded, sending metal shattering across the empty attic, the blast tearing lifts, ropes, cascading them down through the false ceiling onto the still-vacant stage below.

Screams knifed from the tourists just beginning to crowd into the theater.

Dorothy squeaked as she heard the detonation, then ran hard for the exit.

Samothrake took a com from his tuxedo's inner pocket and touched a single sensor.

"All stations, all stations. Begin immediate evacuation of the casino. This is not a drill! Security ... alert the police, advise them bombs have been planted in the casino. I repeat, this is not a drill!"

His voice was still unruffled.

Candia pelted down the dock and jumped down into the *Dolphin*.

Thetis already had the drive on. She cast off the single mooring, reversed away from the dock, and at quarter speed pulled out into the harbor.

Sutro's security element retreated toward the only place they knew to be safe slowly, carefully, skilled combat veterans.

As before, four of the biggest surrounded the fence, while the others leapfrogged each other's movements, guns in their hands, ready.

An old woman saw them, squealed in fear, and limped out of the way.

The men with the guns paid her no mind.

They reached the dock, ran down it. As they did, the lighter's side hatch opened. A man stuck his head out.

"Get the drive started! Some asshole set off a—" Rosser flattened as a metal cylinder tumbled through the air from the lighter. It hit a foot away, bounced, and went off. A thin mist hissed out.

Rosser came to his knees, lifted a gun that was suddenly too heavy, tried to aim at the man in the lighter hatch, and collapsed.

There were other gas grenades rolling around the dock, and men were falling, squirming, then lying motionless.

The two men at the landward end of the dock, rear security, outside the gas's influence, dropped into a kneeling stance. One pulled a wire stock from inside his coat, clipped it to his gun, then went down as a wisp of gas took him.

The other fired, sending a blast of green energy smashing into the empty night, the noise burying the tiny twang of Wolfe's dart gun.

The guard clutched at his throat, tried to find words, half rose, then went down.

Wolfe leapt onto the dock, Libanos behind him, and went to where five men lay. Three were faceup, and he paid them no mind. He rolled the fourth over onto his back and saw the heavy beard. He took out the light and blinked once into the harbor.

He and Libanos dragged the other eight to the lifter, tied them hand and foot, and dumped them into the cargo compartment. Libanos got behind the lighter's controls and keyed switches; the drive surged, and the lifter moved against its moorings.

A few seconds later the *Dolphin* cruised in.

Wolfe picked up Sutro's body, seemingly without effort, carried it to the boat, and slid it down into the stern seat.

He waved to Libanos, who brought the cargo lighter up just clear of the water, spun it, and at half speed headed out of the harbor toward Thrinacia. Wolfe jumped down into the *Dolphin*.

"Any time you're ready," he said.

Thetis gunned the boat away, and the dock was bare and empty, the last gas mist fading against the glare from the casino as firefighters and police vehicles swarmed toward it from ground and air.

* CHAPTER FOURTEEN *

Edet Sutro's body was strapped to a door that had been removed from its hinges and laid across two stone benches in the mansion's wine cellar. Wolfe touched the tip of a spray to Sutro's neck and pressed a stud.

"He'll be back with us shortly," Joshua said. "Candia, would you pack our stuff. We'll be leaving as soon as we finish our chat and Mister Libanos comes back with the lighter."

"How long do we have?" Candia asked.

"You mean before we have to worry about the law? Probably almost forever. Sutro's boys, being illegals, will take a long time to decide it's okay to go legal and holler for help.

"As for the heat themselves—first somebody with the casino will have to make the connection between me and that bomb, which should take three or four days. About that time they'll start checking everybody who has anything to do with the place, and you'll be the only one who turns up missing. Then they'll play connect-the-dots.

"By then we'll be on our third jump out of here, and the Libanoses will have gone to ground wherever they wish.

"Ah. Mister Sutro has returned," he said, seeing the bearded man's eyelids flutter. "Now, if you'll excuse us."

Thetis had been staring fascinatedly at the bound figure. "What are you going to do to him?"

Joshua half smiled. "Very little. Mister Sutro is no fool, and so he'll be more than willing to share a bit of his tawdry past with me."

The girl hesitated and then, at Candia's frown, followed the older woman out and up the stairs. The door closed with a thud.

Sutro's eyes were open, sentience returning.

"Edet, my name is Joshua Wolfe. I know who you are, what you are," the warrant hunter said without preamble.

"You're the gambler that was looking for me," Sutro said.

"I was looking for you. But I'm not a gambler."

"What, then? Law? FI?"

"Let's say ... freelance talent."

"Who are you working for?"

"Since I'm the one who isn't tied up," Wolfe said, "I prefer to ask the questions."

"You won't get any answers."

"Oh, but I shall." Joshua pulled up two empty crates and sat on one. He reached in his pocket, took out the

Lumina, put it on the other crate between the two. Sutro started and then tried to cover it.

"You remember a thief named Innokenty Khodyan?"

Sutro clamped his lips shut. Joshua put a hand on the Lumina, waited until it flamed high, and fixed his stare on Sutro. The man squirmed.

"I do," he said. "He got killed before I could meet him."

"I killed him."

"Ben Greet said he'd been taken by a warrant hunter."

"That's one of my trades."

"There aren't any warrants on me."

"I know that. At least not under the name of Sutro. And I don't have much interest in knowing what your parents tagged you with."

"What do you want to know?"

"Innokenty Khodyan was a pro. He'd hit ten, a dozen worlds, then go to his fence—I don't know if he always used you or if there were others—to dump what he had.

"I'm guessing he mostly worked off tips and the obvious targets.

"He did that on his last run. With one exception. This stone."

"How do you know that?"

"Sutro, I'm not a fool. You're big, you're good, but I don't think even you would know just where to fence an Al'ar Lumina."

Sutro didn't answer.

"You know of a man named Malcolm Penruddock? A retired judge on Mandodari III. Crooked, the word had it. He owned this Lumina, and Innokenty Khodyan took it from him."

"Never heard of him," Sutro said. "I bought from Innokenty, bought almost anything he had. He knew what to steal and what it was worth. He never said anything about that Al'ar rock when he messaged me and said he was ready to sell some things."

"Don't lie, Edet," Wolfe said, his tone mild. "You will not be rewarded in the afterlife.

"Who came to you, told you about Penruddock's Lumina, and said they wanted it?"

Sutro shook his head.

"There's two ways I could go," Wolfe said. "Three, come to think about it. The messy way, which could get bloody and take a while. The Al'ar way . . ."

He picked up the Lumina and held it in front of Sutro's eyes. The man squirmed, trying to pull away from it.

"Let me remind you of something, Edet," Wolfe went on. "I spent six years with the Al'ar. Three as their prisoner . . . and three more before that. Studying their ways.

"Sometimes the Al'ar needed information. Then they'd decide to take a prisoner. You know how often he talked? All the time, Edet. One hundred percent. Of course, he wasn't worth much afterward. The mind didn't come back like it should've.

"Mostly the Al'ar did the merciful thing and killed them. But a few lived. I guess, somewhere back in the Federation, there's probably still a couple of wards full of those people, rotting, dead except their chests move every now and again. We could do it like that, Edet.

"But I'm not as good as the Al'ar. I might get a little sloppy."

He paused. "That's another way. Then there's the sensible way." He set the Lumina to the side. "You tell me what I want to know, and I'll give you something that'll maybe keep *you* alive for a while."

"Right." Sutro sneered. "I go first, of course."

"No," Joshua said. "I'll tell you right now. As I said, this is the sensible way. Penruddock's dead. So's his wife. I was with them when they got killed."

"Why do I care about a couple of bodies I've never even heard of?"

"Lying again, Sutro. Don't do that." Wolfe reached out with a finger and ran it caressingly down behind Sutro's ear and along his jaw line. The bearded man bellowed in agony, his eyes going wide in shock like a poleaxed steer.

Wolfe waited until the man's moans subsided.

"They were killed in sort of an unusual way. Two cargo lighters full of gunsels came in at full tilt, strafed their house, then hauled to the spaceport where their ship was waiting. From there, they vanished like they'd never been.

"I thought that was a little exotic a way to do pay-backs for a little malfeasance in office.

"Now, the interesting thing, and the reason I think he was killed, was I'd shown up on Mandodari III. I was using my real name, which was a mistake. I'm guessing somebody knew who I was, maybe had an ear on Penruddock's com, and didn't want us to get too friendly.

"It takes money to hire a ship and hitters who don't

give a shit if they scatter a few bodies around the land-scape.

"I'd be a little concerned if I were you, Sutro, that maybe your client might want to police up the other end of the connection.

"Now you know what I was going to tell you. You return the favor, I unstrap you, and before we lift I'll drop a call to your goons to come get you.

"Then you'd better think about doing a little running yourself."

Sutro licked his lips, thinking. Wolfe sat completely still.

"All right," the fence said after a time. "I've got no choice, do I? The Lumina *was* a contract job. You're right. I went to Innokenty, gave him the word, told him what it paid.

"It was a lot, Wolfe. Enough for the stupid bastard to just go in, grab the Lumina, and get out.

"But you know crooks. Never steal one thing if they can take a dozen." Sutro tried to shrug but found the straps confining. "Not that I gave a rat's ass. I thought it'd maybe put up a smoke screen."

"So who was the client?"

"You aren't going to believe me. It was the Chitet."

Wolfe tried to cover his reaction but failed.

"That's right," Sutro went on. "Maybe you best take your own advice and think about hatting out of town, eh? Maybe whatever commission you've been offered for whatever you're hunting doesn't look so fat once you realize you're going up against an entire god-damned culture, now, does it?

"Also explains how somebody could afford to hire all those heavies that slotted Penruddock, doesn't it?"

"Thanks for the advice, Edet," Joshua said dryly. "Now get back to the point."

Sutro shrugged. "One of their sobersides came to me, said they wanted something. They, not he. I asked him if he was speaking for the movement or whatever they call themselves. He said as far as I was concerned, yes. Then he told me the details. I told him I didn't know what he was talking about. I wasn't a man who dealt with crooks, let alone jewel thieves. He must be thinking of some other person named Sutro.

"The man just smiled politely and told me ... well, let's say he told me enough about myself so I would've been wasting time playing innocent any longer.

"They had a complete file on Penruddock. Who he was, who his wife was screwing, plans of their house, data about their servants ... everything. The file was like what I'd imagine Federation Intelligence might have."

"What was their price?"

"Ten million credits on delivery. Plus my expenses."

Wolfe lifted an eyebrow. "Penruddock told me he paid only two and a half for it."

"And he was paying top credit. I've seen—heard, actually—of two or three of those things surfacing, and generally they go out for one and a half, maybe two, outside.

"But who was I to tell the Chitet they were wasting their money?"

"What did they want with it?"

"Come on, Wolfe. I wasn't about to ask that kind of question."

"Any theories?"

Sutro shook his head.

"How do you know it was the Chitet? Couldn't it have been maybe a dozen of them who'd decided to go into some kind of business of their own?"

"Could have been," Sutro said. "But I don't think so. I was given a complete list of com sites to use if there were any problems. There were places on ten, a dozen worlds, plus some blankies I don't know where."

"So you were briefed, and I assume they gave you a retainer. How big?"

"A mill."

"That tends to make you take people seriously. What came next?"

"I went to Innokenty and put him in motion."

"Then what?"

"I waited."

"Did you have any further contact with the Chitet?"

"That was the only physical contact I had and the only Chitet I ever met. Although he had four security types with him. All dressed like they always do, like they're damned religious caterpillars."

"While Innokenty Khodyan was off being a villain, did they contact you?"

"Two, maybe three times."

"How impatient were they?"

"I couldn't tell. They were always calm, always quiet. I'd never had anything to do with them before, just read about them. They behaved just like I'd imagined they would."

"What happened when things went wrong and you found out Innokenty Khodyan was dead and the Lumina was gone?"

"I contacted the main number they'd given me and talked to the voice there. They never turned their vid pickup on. And it always sounded like the same voice."

"How'd he take it?"

"Weird," Sutro said. "I could have been talking about the weather. I had the strange notion that if I'd said I had the Lumina in my hand, I would've gotten the same no-bother comeback, as well."

"How did they end it?"

"That was strange, too. I was told I could keep the retainer, and possibly I would be dealing with them again in the future. They told me to dump all the information I had, though. They'd come to me."

"So where's the list of com sites?"

"Wolfe, as you said, I'm no fool. When Ben Greet said Innokenty had been nailed by the law, I jumped out of there and reported. I would have blanked my data even if they hadn't told me to. I've stayed clean because I stay clean."

Wolfe considered for a moment, then loosened Sutro's straps and pulled one arm free. He picked up the Lumina and held it out.

"Edet, touch the stone."

Sutro hesitated.

"Go ahead. Nothing'll happen to you."

Reluctantly the fence obeyed. Once more the stone flamed colors. Wolfe closed his eyes, appeared to listen, then set the Lumina down and refastened Sutro's bonds.

"All right. If you're lying, you're lying to yourself, too."

"That's all?"

"Not quite. Now, you're going to go through every detail, as it happened, from the time the Chitet came to you, what these men looked like, and everything else until you dumped your files."

"There he comes," Thetis said. "See? From just behind that island five points off north."

The lighter was a white dot against the blue water and sped toward the island at high speed, not more than two yards above the water, foam frothing up on either side of the hull.

Joshua and Candia's travel cases were stacked on the verandah, and Thetis sat on one of them.

The lighter slowed as it neared the beach. But instead of berthing at the pier, it cut its drive, skewed sideways, and settled down into the water about thirty yards offshore. The front hatch lifted.

"Get down," Joshua snapped, pulling Candia sprawling behind one of the cases, then yanking Thetis to the cover of one of the verandah's columns. Bewildered, she crouched. A gun appeared in Joshua's hand.

A man stood in the lighter's hatch. He was not Jacob Libanos. In spite of the heat, he wore sober, dark clothing. He had a neat goatee. A man and a woman appeared beside him. One was Libanos. The woman, dressed in quiet, subdued clothing, held a gun against the old man's side.

A loudspeaker crackled.

"Joshua Wolfe. Please surrender. We do not wish to

provoke bloodshed. We know you have the man named Sutro, and we wish to talk to both of you. Do not force us to take physical action."

"Bastard," Joshua swore, then regained control. "Candia, you and Thetis go out the back. Try to find a place to hide. I'll try to stall them. They shouldn't look for you too hard."

"Joshua Wolfe," the voice came again. "Please come into the open with your hands raised. Tell the others in your party to do the same, or else Libanos will be shot. This is not an empty threat."

"Go on, you two!" Joshua said.

"No." The voice belonged to Thetis.

Joshua turned his head. She had her small pistol out, aimed at his head.

"No," she said again. "We do just what that man wants."

"Thetis—"

"That's my grandfather! Do what I said!" Her voice was shaking, but it was very determined. Candia started to say something.

"Shut up," Thetis snapped.

Joshua stared at her, then grunted, spun his pistol out into the open, and stood, lifting his hands.

The two men pushed Joshua into the room. He stumbled, nearly went down, regained his balance. He was naked and blindfolded.

He *felt* four others in the room, but none of them spoke. After a moment a woman laughed deliberately. For a moment Joshua felt comfortable. That was very much part of the familiar basics of interrogation.

The woman spoke. "Is it agreed that I speak for the Order?"

Three voices agreed.

"Joshua Wolfe, we desire certain information from you. It is expected that you will not cooperate. Unfortunately, we have but a limited period of time to secure this data, and so we shall be forced to use methods that are normally abhorrent to us, save in the most extreme cases.

"This is such a time."

Wolfe barely had time to sense the blow before it hammered into his diaphragm. He gasped and staggered, and he was hit twice more, once in the kidneys, then in the side of the head.

He went down, curled, protecting his privates, smelling pine oil from the floor, tasting blood and vomit in the back of his throat.

A kick thudded into his back, another into his ribs. A hand grabbed his neck and twisted it, and three times a fist smashed into his face.

"That is enough. Remove him," the woman said.

This time Joshua had been permitted to wear a thin pair of pajama pants that might once have been white but now were soiled with bloodstains, filth, and dried excrement, none of it his. His eyes were uncovered.

He was pulled from the room they'd picked for his cell, a large, windowless storage room at the back of the mansion. He had no idea where the others were.

One man held a blaster on him; the other two strapped his hands behind his back with plas restrainers. They frog-marched him down the corridor into what had been the dining room. Wolfe saw his own blood-stains on the polished wooden floor. Now the windows had been covered, and the long table had been moved to the side. There were four chairs behind it. Two of them were occupied, one by a woman, not unattractive, in her thirties, hair worn in a convenient pageboy cut. The man was some years older, with gray close-cut hair and a neat goatee. Both wore quiet clothing that came close to being a uniform. There was a gun on the table in front of the woman.

Two of the guards left. The one who remained was squat and heavy-muscled, with narrow eyes that never left Wolfe.

"Is it agreed that I speak for the Order?" the woman said, no question in her voice.

"It is."

"Joshua Wolfe, I require you to answer certain questions. You will answer them fully and completely."

"To whom am I speaking?"

"You may call me Bori. It is not my name but will give you a symbol to use."

"Where are my friends?"

"They are still alive and are being kept secure. You should be aware that their safety depends on your coop-eration, of course."

"When you have what you need, what do you intend doing?"

"I do not think that pertains to the moment," Bori said. "I am the one with the questions."

Wolfe half smiled.

"You find something funny?"

"I was just remembering something I told Sutro a few hours ago."

"We know a great deal about you, Joshua Wolfe. About your war record, about your time with the Al'ar, even your activities here in the Outlaw Worlds, although you've done an excellent job of remaining nearly invisible."

"Since you know everything, then what's the point of our . . . chatting?"

"Tyrma!"

The squat man slashed a knife hand sideways into Wolfe's upper arm. Joshua winced and bit his lip to keep from crying out.

"We have little time or appreciation for humor," Bori said. "Now, you will please answer our questions. First, the most immediate matters:

"Are there other bombs set in the casino, as the police believe?"

"No."

"The reason we asked was because if there was going to be further upset to the order of things, it might be well to immediately go offworld before continuing our interrogation. I suspect you are telling the truth and that first bomb was merely to create a diversion.

"Do you have other associates beyond the ones we secured?"

"No."

"Where is your ship?"

"Offworld. In a parking orbit."

"Then you lied. There *are* others in your team."

Tyrma struck again, this time with a side kick to Wolfe's ankle. Joshua almost fell, recovered.

"How many are there in your crew?"

"Two," Wolfe said.

"How will you summon them?" Bori held up the bonemike from Wolfe's gear, and he experienced a faint moment of hope. "This device appears of too limited a range to reach beyond the planetary surface."

"I use a conventional com," he said. "I place a call through the offworld connection to a certain party on a certain world on a certain link. My ship's computer monitors any com that's broadcast of that nature, and the crew'll land at whatever point I told them to.

"If the pickup point has changed, then I can use any microwave transmitter to tell them where to get me once they're in-atmosphere."

"Complicated," Bori said. "But careful, so I am not surprised. We shall require you at a certain time to summon them.

"But not at the moment.

"Who are you working for?"

Joshua said nothing, stiffening for the blow.

"No, Tyrma. Not now. We shall outline our needs to Joshua Wolfe before we apply further stress.

"Are you working for the Federation? Specifically, are you working for Federation Intelligence? If so, we shall need to know all the details of your mission, including controlling agents and when and how you report.

"Are you working for the Outlaw Worlds' own law enforcement?

"Are you working on a matter of personal concern?"

"I'm following my own trail."

"Which is?"

"When the Al'ar trained me, they used a Lumina stone," Wolfe said. "When I served the warrant on Innokenty Khodyan, I discovered the stone.

"I wanted to know where it came from and where I could find others. That is why I went to Penruddock."

Bori stared at him, reached under the table, took out the Lumina, and set it in front of her. "We shall return to that line of questioning again. I am not sure I accept your story."

Joshua waited.

"There are stories that not all the Al'ar departed . . . or did whatever they did at the end of the war. Have you heard such tales?"

"I have."

"Do you believe them?"

"No. I checked on a few of them, found they were gas."

"We are fairly sure you are wrong," Bori said. "Next question: Have you ever heard of the Mother Lumina? Perhaps you would have known it as the Overlord Stone. It would have been some sort of controlling or recording device for all Luminas, perhaps."

"No."

Bori considered. "I am not sure I accept that answer, either. We shall ask it again . . . under different circumstances.

"What do you know of the Secrets of the Al'ar?"

Wolfe lifted an eyebrow. "Bori, are the Chitet going mad? Secrets of the Al'ar? Like what? Like where they went?"

"Tyrma!"

Again the squat man struck Joshua.

"I was referring to the curiosity show called *The Secrets of the Al'ar*. It is scheduled to perform, or do whatever it does, in a few weeks here on Trinité. It also appeared on Mandodari III not long before we learned, through some of our friends who have not yet joined us openly, of Judge Penruddock's acquisition of the Lumina.

"We are wondering if this is a coincidence or not. We have, as a matter of course, close-sieved *all* matters dealing with the Al'ar."

"The first I heard of it was seeing something on my com after I landed," Joshua said. "I don't know anything about it other than it sounds like a freak show."

"Let me ask you something," he continued. "If your pet goon won't flatten me for it. What do the Chitet want with Luminas?"

"We do not particularly care about this stone or the others that have surfaced. However, there are matters far bigger and more sensitive behind them that we must deal with. We believe our duty is to all humanity, and we know, and you need not ask how, that the matter of the Al'ar is *not* over and settled.

"I will not explain further, except that the questions I have must and shall be answered and answered truthfully."

"And then what happens?"

"To you? We shall give you a quick and painless death. It is necessary. At one time, perhaps even after the war, you had ties with Federation Intelligence. They must not learn of the Chitet's activities.

"As for your companions . . . we haven't decided what logic dictates must happen."

"You sure give me a lot of encouragement."

"Oh, but we do, Joshua Wolfe. It has been a long time since the war, and perhaps you forget just how wonderful the thought of death ending agony can be.

"Return him to his room. Deal with him as I ordered."

Tyrma jerked Wolfe toward the door.

In the cell he and one other guard coldly beat Wolfe into unconsciousness while the third man kept his gun ready.

It was hot, hot like a fever dream, when Joshua came back to awareness. The light glared down at him.

He tried to clear his muzzy head, looked about for water.

There was none.

A man's agonized screams sounded, and Joshua thought that might have been what had brought him back to awareness.

He thought the screams came from Sutro.

After a moment, his head lolled and he heard no more.

Again he woke, with no idea of how long he had been senseless.

Again he heard screams.

A woman's voice.

"No. Please. Don't do that to me. Not again. Please. Oh, gods, it hurts too much!"

The words faded into agonized cries for mercy that would not be granted.

The voice was Candia's. Then came a man's guttural laughter.

Wolfe staggered to his feet, stumbled to the door, was about to pull at it, then caught himself.

Breathe . . . breathe . . . the earth reaches out, holds you . . . slowly . . .

His hands moved in patterns through the air for a time. Then he went back to the far wall and sat down. His expression was calm.

"It is not working," the technician said. "The sensors in his clothing show complete normalcy, tranquility."

"Shut it off," Bori said.

The technician touched a sensor, and the screams ended as the voice synthesizer shut off.

"We shall try another method," she said. She seemed undisturbed.

Wolfe's body contorted against the straps, his face writhing in pain. There were tiny receivers hooked to his nipples and his lower legs.

"It is a simple matter for the pain to stop," Bori said, her voice sympathetic, friendly. "All I need is what you know, and then all of this shall go away, and you will be given water, food, be allowed to sleep.

"Or I can increase the level of pain. Or move the receptors. Men have far more sensitive areas than the ones I am currently having stimulated."

Breathe . . . breathe . . .

She motioned, and the tech moved a slidepot.

Again Wolfe shuddered, then his body went limp, his expression still.

"Shut it down!" For the first time urgency entered Bori's voice.

The technician obeyed.

"Does he have a suicide block?"

The tech looked at another machine.

"I don't know," the man said. "I can't tell. But he's under some sort of control. Look, here on the screen. All synapses were responding as a normal human male should under the applied stimuli, then suddenly it stopped . . . *before* you ordered me to!"

Bori thought for a time.

"Disconnect him. We cannot take the chance of finding out what kind of mind/body power he is using.

"Would drugs be an option?"

"I'm not sure," the technician said. "We couldn't just hit him with a hard dose. I'll bet the same thing would happen. Maybe if we started with a small dose, then worked our way up . . . maybe."

Bori turned to Tyrma, who stood behind her. "You saw what happened. Physical stress techniques, whether like this or of the sort you are trained to practice, will be of no benefit. I'll devise another approach."

The squat man looked disappointed.

Tyrma and the two guards woke Joshua Wolfe from his stupor and dragged him out of his room and through the ruins of the mansion's living area.

Wolfe wondered what they'd been looking for, decided anything, and concentrated on what would happen next. *Breathe* . . .

Waiting on the dock were Candia, Thetis, her grandfather, Sutro, Bori, the goateed man, and two other Chitet. All the Chitet wore holstered guns.

Wolfe noted that a starship lay in the shallows about fifty yards away and that the hatch was open.

The guards marched Wolfe out onto the pier. He could feel the hot boards under his feet, feel them creak as he walked, and he could smell the sunlight.

"Joshua Wolfe," Bori began. "You appear to be impervious to most conventional questioning methods, and we do not have the time for further delays. Nor can we chance taking you offworld with us. Therefore, I am giving you one final option:

"Tell us what you know, now, or else your companions will die one by one."

"Not my granddaughter," Libanos bellowed, lowering his head, hands stretching for Bori. A guard had his pistol out and snapped its barrel against the back of his neck. Libanos's knees caved, and he slumped to the dock.

Melting . . .

"Will you talk?" Bori drew her gun.

Wolfe did not answer or move.

"We shall start with the least important, to prove our . . . sincerity, if you will."

Sutro had time to bring up his hands, shielding his face, before Bori shot him neatly in midchest. The blaster made a half-inch hole in his chest and blew most of his back in a bloody spray across the water. Sutro fell back, splashed into the crystalline ocean, lay motionless. The water around him turned brown, then red.

"Will you talk?"

Again Wolfe made no reply.

The air takes me . . .

The gun swung to Thetis. She flinched, waiting for the blow she'd never feel.

Tyrma shouted a warning in an unknown language.

For an instant Joshua Wolfe was not there but was a shimmer in the soft tropical air.

Bori's fingers touched the trigger stud far too late. The bolt crashed out into the ocean.

Tyrma was the first to die. Wolfe temple struck him, then tapped his chest with the heel of his hand; he *felt* the squat man's heart stop and shoved the falling corpse into Bori, who stumbled back, dropping her gun, almost going into the water.

The guards behind Wolfe fumbled for their pistols. Joshua moved easily, without hurry, a blur, around the first one's side, blocking the second's aim; he drove a knife hand into the first guard's carotid and never heard him gurgle death as Libanos, still lying on the boards, swept the second guard's feet from under him, roaring, grabbing the Chitet in his great old, strangling bear hands.

Bori was scrabbling for her gun, and Thetis kicked her, sending her sprawling onto her back. The woman rolled as she hit, had Thetis's foot, twisted it, and sent the girl spinning, crying out in pain.

The goateed man's gun was lifting as Wolfe came in on him; a fist smash into his biceps paralyzed his arm, sending the pistol clattering to the decking. Wolfe's hand curled oddly, cobra touch, and darted into the base of the goateed man's throat. He tried to scream and sprayed blood through his shattered larynx for an instant before Wolfe's forearm jolted up, snapping his neck.

A blaster went off, blowing a hole into the deck as Candia kicked out, a dancer's kick, and knocked the gunman into the water.

The last guard's fingers opened nervelessly, his eyes cavernous as the world changed about him, and his mouth opened, perhaps to cry for help, as Libanos shot him in the face.

Bori was the only Chitet left alive on the dock. Wolfe could hear shouts of alarm from the ship's open hatchway but paid them no mind.

The woman rolled to her feet in an attack stance, facing him. Her face was as it always had been, calm, controlled, and then most of her head vanished as Thetis shot her once, then again in the body with her own pistol.

"The house," Wolfe shouted. He scooped up two of the pistols and shot the guard in the water who was floundering toward the ship, and they went running down the dock as a bolt impacted in the water beside them, steam boiling, curling in the clear air.

Wolfe knelt, aimed, weak hand curled around his gun butt, touched the stud, and blasted a smoking hole inside the Chitet ship's lock. Then he ran after the others.

Libanos was overturning couches, pulling tables up for barricades. Joshua paid no mind, running into the mansion's dining room.

The Lumina was still sitting on the middle of the table. Wolfe went around the table, saw his bonemike on the floor behind the chair, grabbed it.

"Ship!"

"I hear."

"All systems full alert! Lift! Weapons station, full readiness."

"Understood."

"I will correct. Fire when you clear the water."

"Understood."

He pocketed the Lumina, ran back to the mansion's living room, and peered through one of the windows. He saw a pod on the starship opening, speedboat on davits, Chitet with rifles getting into it.

A blaster bolt shattered a column outside, and Wolfe ducked back.

Then the ocean boiled, and his ship lifted off the sea floor and broke the surface, water streaming from it. A concealed bay slid open, and the chaingun emerged.

"Target ... starship. Two-second burst, directly into the air lock."

"Understood."

The dragon roared, and fire spit from the multiple muzzles of the gun, searing like a cutting torch through the unarmored Chitet ship, then shifting aim, and a thousand more three-quarter-inch-diameter collapsed-uranium rounds ripped through the lock door.

The starship rolled on its side, and flames spurted.

"Pickup!"

"Understood."

The ship moved over the water and across the sand, crushing the gazebo as it hovered closer.

"Open the lock."

The lock door opened, and a ramp shot out.

Wolfe had Candia by the arm, pulling her toward the

ship. Libanos scooped up his granddaughter and, puffing heavily, followed.

They clattered up the ramp, and it slid closed behind them.

"Straight up," Wolfe snapped. "Get us out-atmosphere."

"Understood."

The *Grayle* stood on its tail, and its drive tubes hummed.

Flames mushroomed from the Chitet ship's lock. A moment later the ship exploded. A ball of black and gray, red-streaked, climbed toward the *Grayle*, but not fast enough as it soared toward space.

* CHAPTER FIFTEEN *

Thetis stared, fascinated, at her index finger. She crooked it.

"I never thought," she said slowly, "I'd ever kill anyone. Or how easy it is." She moved her finger once more.

Wolfe looked at Libanos. The four of them stood on the *Grayle*'s loading platform. Tied up to it was a double-hulled boat older than Joshua, its purpose obvious to anyone half a mile downwind.

Libanos touched his mustache. "I don't know," he said. "I got over it." He sighed. "But I think I left something behind."

"We all did," Wolfe said quietly.

Thetis looked up. "I'll be all right, Grandfather. It's just . . . maybe I've led too sheltered a life."

"Go back to it," Candia said. "Sometimes the wild side isn't the best."

Thetis reached out and took her hand. "Thanks. I'm

sorry about the things . . . the things maybe I thought."
She blushed and jumped down into the fishing boat.

Joshua handed Libanos a thick plas envelope. The old
man opened it, saw the credits, and stuffed the envelope
inside his shirt.

"What are you going to do next?" Wolfe asked.

"First thing is to have Marf, here, run us back to
Morne-des-Esses and find out, real loud, that while we
were off helpin' him pull his nets, some cheap pricks
stole Thetis's boat.

"After that . . . well, I guess I'll close down the house
for a while, maybe go sail around the islands in an old
hooker I've got moored outside Diamant, and start
lookin' for wood to put up and season for the new boat.

"Read some, think some.

"There's a fishin' village on one of the out islands I
may port out of for a while. There was a little boy Thetis was sweet on six, seven years ago. Maybe she'd like
to see what he grew up like.

"Then I'll put in for victims' relief and start thinking
about rebuilding the *Dolphin*. There's a few things I
didn't do quite right the first time around.

"I'll stay out of the line of fire for a while, until this
settles."

"Good," Joshua said.

"How big a stink is this going to make?"

"Big," Joshua said flatly. "Explosion in a casino . . .
an island about volcanoed when a starship blew up . . .
if they run DNA traces, there'll be a pile of bodies to
think about. But I think all they'll be looking for is a
gambler named Wolfe and his dancer friend."

"Wasn't concerned about the proper authorities,"

Libanos grunted. "Day I can't make them dance my tune without knowin' they're jiggin' is the day I'll be ready for the long count.

"I was thinkin' of your friends the Chitet."

"They didn't make a full report," Joshua said. "Not after they arrived here. My ship was monitoring all freqs, and there weren't any out-system coms outside of Wule and Diamant. You should be clean."

"Let's hope, anyway." Libanos hesitated. "Do me a favor, Mister Wolfe. Don't come back anytime soon, hear? Life gets a little exciting with you about.

"A little too exciting."

As they turned back to the *Grayle*, Wolfe noticed that Candia was looking at him oddly.

"You're sure the dancer didn't have any idea you're on a contract for us?" Cisco asked.

"Positive," Wolfe said.

"So where'd you leave her?"

"I don't think you need to know that. Somewhere she'll be safe. Somewhere quiet. She said she thought she'd like to try a little quieter life by herself. She said . . . things had changed." Wolfe tried to smile but didn't quite manage it. "Cisco, drop her, all right? She's not a player. I want to know how many goddamned Chitet there are, and you keep ducking the question! How far do I have to run, how deep a hole do I have to dig, how many cubic feet of dirt do I have to pull in after me?"

Cisco considered his words. "We don't know."

"What do you mean? How many worlds do they have . . . how many ships . . . how many people? Those are pretty simple matters. And what in the hell are they doing icing people for these goddamned Luminas? What do they care about the Al'ar? Or doesn't Federation Intelligence know that, either?"

"We know the size of their culture. But we don't know how many of them have gone outlaw or what they want."

Wolfe blinked. "Wait a minute. What do you mean, outlaw? I surely got the idea the woman who called herself Bori was speaking for the entire movement or culture or whatever the hell it's calling itself."

"We think differently," Cisco said.

"Why?"

"I can't tell you. To be honest, I don't know myself. All I know is I got the word, from people who're far higher in the directorate than I am, that there's only a few renegades who're calling themselves Chitet, and we're already in the process of rounding them up. We're just giving them a little time and a little rope until we make sure we've got all of them in the net.

"The main Chitet culture is just what it's always been. That's an absolute."

"So one of your boys called whoever speaks for all the Order, and he said cross his heart, we're all just reputable citizens, eh? About the level of analysis FI usually does."

Cisco made no response. Wolfe looked hard into his eyes. The intelligence executive met and held his gaze. Wolfe began to ask another question but changed his mind.

"But that doesn't alter the problem I've got," he said

instead. "It only takes one of them and one gun and I'm history."

"You're under our cover, Wolfe. Don't worry about them. I've already put the word out, and they'll be dealt with. They won't have time to be messing with you."

Wolfe looked unconvinced.

"But that wasn't why I wanted a face-to-face," Cisco said. He got up, walked to one of the *Grayle*'s screens, and looked at the huge bulk of the Federation frigate that lay half a mile distant, outlined by far-distant stars. Then he turned back.

"The contract has changed," he said.

"To what?"

"We've had further developments I'm not able to tell you about. We're doubling the fee, and I'll give you some numbers that you can use to get whatever backup you need, anytime, anywhere.

"When you find the Al'ar, you're to take him out."

Wolfe was on his feet. "The hell I will! I'm not one of your goddamned assassins!"

"You've done it before."

"That was a long time ago!"

Cisco grimaced. "I'm sorry you feel like that. You know, if I'd had done to me what those bastards did to you, I'd be more than happy to put the last one in his meat crate."

"You're you," Wolfe said. "No deal."

"You aren't being asked, Joshua."

"And if I tell you to shove it, I'll be out in the open for the Chitet?"

"That," Cisco said carefully, "and very conceivably

worse. You don't need FI for an enemy, even out here in the Outlaw Worlds."

Wolfe stared at him once more, and this time the man looked away.

"Get off my ship," Wolfe said, his voice calm.

"You'll keep the contract?"

"You heard me."

Cisco took a microfiche from his pocket and set it down on the panel next to him. "Here's the contact numbers you might need. You've also got open call on any FI warships in your area if it gets that bad." He went to the open lock door and started to wriggle into his suit. Wolfe followed him, watched, made no move to help.

Cisco's gauntleted hand was about to snap the faceplate closed, when he paused.

"I'd say I'm sorry, Wolfe. But this whole thing is big and getting bigger. None of us has any choice. Come on, man! This is for the Federation!"

Wolfe made no response. Cisco snapped the plate closed and touched a sensor on the hull. The inner lock door irised shut.

Joshua waited until he heard the outer lock cycle open, then went to a screen and watched Cisco being reeled across space toward the Federation warship's yawning lock.

He thought about what Cisco had just said and wondered again who in the government was so interested in Luminas.

"The question is really, I suppose," he said, "how many Chitet are inside Federation Intelligence?"

* * *

"I see," Joshua said thoughtfully. "So you really don't have any way of knowing when I could book *The Secrets of the Al'ar*."

He waited while his words and image jumped through several subspace transponder units to the screen on the harried-looking woman's littered desk.

"Not really," she answered. "I'm afraid Mister Javits is, shall we say, a bit eccentric. Perhaps that's why he chose to use my agency instead of one of the larger ones.

"All I can do is list your number and Carlton VI, and when Mister Javits contacts me, which he does on a regular basis, I'll inform him of your interest. Then I'll get back to you and we can arrange a contract, security deposits, and so forth.

"Certainly it should be no longer than an E-month, perhaps two. But in the interim," the woman went on, "you have the show's past itinerary, and you're more than welcome to check with any of the promoters who've booked *The Secrets*. It's one of my most popular attractions."

"I'd also like to see the show myself," Wolfe said. "I've had friends who caught it, but I've learned to never book anything I'm not really enthusiastic about myself."

"I'll upload the current tour schedule right now," the agent said. "Mister Javits—I've never met him, never even seen him—seems to always be on the road." She giggled. "Now, isn't that funny that we still say that?"

"It's better than saying 'on the ether,' " Wolfe said, "or 'on the hyperspace' and sound like Space Rangers of the Galaxy."

"I guess so." The woman fingered sensors on her keyboard. "There. It's on its way. Oh, wait. One change that won't appear on what you're getting.

"*The Secrets was* booked onto Trinité," she said. "Mister Javits canceled that just two days ago."

"Oh? Why?"

"He said he has a friend there who told him advance sales and interest weren't promising. He also said there was an outbreak of some rather worrisome virus in the capital, which is, umm, Diamant, which he'd as soon not chance catching.

"But he does that very, very seldom, so you needn't worry, since I know you'll do an excellent job of four-walling."

"I hope so. One further question. How many people does Mister Javits use on his tour? I'd like to know that so I can plan lodgings and so forth."

"To be honest, I don't know that myself. I've only seen holos of the presentation. But you needn't worry about putting people up. The show is entirely self-contained. It's very automated, which is another of the attractions, especially for the younger set.

"All you need provide is an open area, permission from your local authorities for Mister Javits's ship to port there and remain during the duration of the performances, and he'll set up everything else, including a good-sized weatherproofed arena he carries aboard ship. He's a *very* sophisticated showman.

"Thank you for your interest and time, Mister Hunt," the woman said. "I'm sure you'll be delighted you decided to book *The Secrets of the Al'ar*."

"I'm sure I shall."

The screen blanked, and Wolfe's polite smile vanished.

"So how did I avoid catching this mysterious virus?" he said thoughtfully. "And isn't Mister Javits just the careful one?

"Ship, we're going to do some plotting. Stand by."

"So *The Secrets* did play Mandodari, like Bori said," Wolfe mused. "Now overlay the FI projections on where the other four Lumina first surfaced on top of the old schedule."

"Done."

"Any correlation?"

"None within your parameters."

"Dammit!" Wolfe stood, stretched, walked to one wall, and opened a panel. He looked at the array of bottles inside, picked up a bottle of Laberdolive, read the label twice, replaced it, and closed the panel. He went to a second panel, opened the refrigerator door it concealed, took out a bottle of mineral water, and drank.

"Wait a minute. How long after *The Secrets* show played Mandodari VI did Penruddock report his Lumina stolen?"

"Nearly a year."

"Extend my time parameter to a year between the Luminas' appearance and the tour. Now is there anything?"

"All four appearances now coincide."

"Well, hot damn. I think we're getting somewhere. Now overlay the Al'ar capital worlds and the show's previous appearances. Any conjunction?"

"Yes, on five."

"Including Sauros, where somebody filmed that Al'ar?"

"Including Sauros."

"As a matter of curiosity, is there one of the Al'ar capital worlds within reach of Trinité?"

"Affirmative. Estimated orbit . . . two jumps. Ship time, four days."

"But the Chitet and I messed up that one," Wolfe said. "Now, take the current tour and plot Al'ar capital worlds around it."

"Done."

"How many match?"

"All of them."

"Mister Javits, you aren't *that* careful. What's the nearest one we can reach in time to see the show?"

"The nearest is Montana Keep. Estimated jumps . . . six. Internal time . . . two ship weeks. Date of appearance . . . three E-weeks. The Secrets of the Al'ar is booked to appear there for two full local weeks."

"Make the jumps."

Joshua remembered a painting. It had gone with his family on all of its assignments and was generally hung just inside the front entrance to their residences. The reproduction was a simple picture showing a clown and a young woman staring at him, an odd expression on her face. The boy had spent hours staring at it, imagining what had happened, who the two were, and what they meant to each other.

The painting crashed to the floor, and the Al'ar soldier's booted heel smashed down on it.

He spoke into a microphone, and a cold synthesized

voice came from the small box on his weapons belt: "Come now or face death! Take only what you are wearing! Nothing else is permitted!"

Joshua's father tried to protest, and one of the soldier's companions backhanded him. His mother screamed then and was seized by two more of the squad.

Joshua took one step forward, and three slender gun muzzles aimed steadily at his chest.

"Young one, move no farther or you will die," the soldier in charge ordered.

As the Al'ar hurried them down the embassy steps, flames roared from the back of the building.

Two of the Marine guards and their sergeant lay dead in front of the building.

Something else rose in Joshua's memory.

A man's white, pale hand sticking out of the dirt, an ornate, old-fashioned signet ring on one finger. Joshua stooped, slipped the ring off his father's hand, stood. He took a deep breath, picked up the shovel, and finished filling in the grave.

He turned to his mother and gave her the ring.

"Do we say a prayer or something?"

"Who do we pray to?" she asked harshly. "Can you think of a god worth the words?"

He shook his head and took her arm, and they walked away, past the long lines of mounded earth in the camp's graveyard.

Then he remembered coming back from a work detail and seeing four men outside the hut he and his mother shared.

"Don't go in there, boy. Your mother died about an hour ago. We just buried her."

It was harsh, but it was the camp way.

Joshua shook his head, disbelieving. "But she was able to sit up this morning! I fed her some broth."

None of the men answered.

Joshua managed a breath through frozen lungs. "What did you do with the ring she had? It was my father's."

"We didn't find anything like that, son," one of the men said, trying to sound kind. Joshua knew he was lying.

Wolfe got up suddenly from the control chair and walked down the spiral steps and into the ship's kitchen.

Very deliberately, concentrating only on what his hands were doing, he began making a pot of tea.

The mirrors of the workout room reflected two stools. On one sat the Lumina, flaming brilliantly. On the second was a ripe multistriped melon.

The stone "burned" higher, and then, for an instant, there was the blink of a hand extending, fingers held together in a knife thrust.

The tips of the fingers barely touched the melon, and it exploded, spraying juice and pulp across the room.

Joshua Wolfe was suddenly visible in the mirrors.

He stared at the shattered fruit, nodded once, and began to clean up the mess.

* CHAPTER SIXTEEN *

BOMBS ROCK
LUXURY HOTEL

1 Killed as Blasts
Shatter Penthouse

Press for More

Two bombs exploded just after dusk today in two floors of Carlton VI's most luxurious hotel, the Hyland Central, killing one hotel employee.

Police are seeking the leaseholder of the hotel's penthouse to aid in their inquiries.

Dead was Peter Lough-ran, 45, a longtime employee of the hotel assigned to the night security detail.

Police bomb experts said the twin devices were professionally made and set. The lieutenant in charge, whose name by government policy cannot be revealed, said,

"It appears the first bomb went off in the Hyland's penthouse and was triggered by Mister Loughran, making a routine check of the apartments as ordered by the penthouse's tenant."

"A few moments later," the lieutenant continued, "a second bomb, obviously linked to the first, destroyed a smaller room two stories below."

Police theorize that the penthouse's leaseholder, Mister Joshua Wolfe, was the target of the attack and the bomb was inadvertently set off by Mister Loughran.

The purpose of the second bomb is unknown at this time, and the room's occupant, a Mister Samuel Baker, who held the room on a long-term lease, is being sought for questioning.

Damage to the hotel was extensive and will require rebuilding of both floors the devices were detonated on.

Little information was available on Mister Wolfe at press time. He was considered a model tenant who kept to himself and never caused trouble. Hotel records as to his profession and employment were non-existent, however, which has aroused police suspicions. He is currently believed to be offworld.

Mister Baker was unknown to any of the hotel employees, and no information whatsoever appears available. The relationship between the two men, if any, is also unknown.

Anyone with information as to the whereabouts of either of these men should contact Carlton VI planetary police at C-8788-6823-6789.

* * *

34ERS 45MCS MDU89 QZ3RE . . . IT IS IMPERATIVE YOU COMMUNICATE SOONEST WITH YOUR STATUS, CURRENT DESTINATION, AND ANY FURTHER DATA WHICH MAY BE USEFUL, SO MAXIMUM FEDERATION SUPPORT CAN BE MADE AVAILABLE.

CISCO

"Standing by for response."

"There won't be any."

Joshua crumpled the page from the one-time pad and pushed it into the trash destructor slot, then turned to the screen with the contract he'd been studying when Cisco's message came in.

"And they say there's no such thing as slavery any more," he finally murmured. He picked up the lightpen and signed it: Ed Hunt. Then he touched the TRANSMIT sensor.

"Hi-ho. Hi-ho. It's off to work we go."

* CHAPTER SEVENTEEN *

Steam clouds hissed up and grew larger as the cargo ship's drive nudged it toward the yellow pillars that marched from the shore deep into the jungle.

"All contract workers, Lock Bravo for immediate disembarking. This is the last call."

The ship nosed up to the floating dock below the structure, and magnetic grapples clanged. The ship rolled slightly in the sullen surf that washed up on the beach about a hundred yards away.

The ship's lock extended out over the dock, and the portal irised open. The half a hundred men waiting inside tasted the world's air. It was humid, sticky, threatening.

"Lumberpigs first, old lags second, virgins last," someone shouted. Men picked up their duffels and made their way up the lighter's ramp to the dock and into an elevator.

Joshua slung his carryall over one shoulder, then bent to pick up the square leather-bound case beside him. A dark man who'd been in the same compartment with Wolfe in the short jump from Lectat IV to Montana Keep grabbed the case's handles and lifted.

"Jesu, buddy, what the hell you got in there? Rocks?"

"Books," Joshua said.

"A reader, eh? Be interestin' to see if you can stay awake long enough offshift t' turn a page. I never can." The man shouldered his own gear, and the two joined the line snaking off the craft.

A man wearing a protective helmet and an officious expression waited on the dock. He held a notebook and checked names as the men went past.

"Virgins, over here. All new hires, let's go. Come on, virgins," he said monotonously. Wolfe stepped out of line, nodding good-bye to his acquaintance.

"See you up the Centipede," the man said, and disappeared into an elevator.

"Name," the helmeted man said.

"Hunt," Joshua said. "Ed Hunt."

The man keyed sensors. "Right. You're unassigned, right?"

"Right."

"Go topside, second companionway to the right, down two levels. Personnel will plug you in."

Joshua started away.

"Hang on." The man took a sensor from his back pocket. "I'm assumin' you followed orders and didn't bring any hooch or high, right?"

"I don't get cooked on the job."

"Yeh," the man said, disbelieving. "Nobody does. That's why we don't gotta shake all you lice down to keep you from gettin' fried and fallin' in the scaler." He ran the sensor up and down Joshua's body. "You're clean. Open the bags."

Joshua opened the carryall. The man probed through it, found nothing. He opened the leather-bound case, then hesitated. He looked up and met Joshua's steady gaze. The man looked puzzled for an instant, then shook his head and closed the case without examining it.

" 'Kay. You ain't carryin' nothing. Go on or you'll be late for noon meal."

Joshua went into an elevator, rode it to the top, and stepped out onto the structure's flat deck.

It curled from the shore two miles into the jungle, more than four hundred feet above the jungle floor, and was made of a series of cylindrically legged segments. The deck under him hummed from hidden machinery. Each segment's top deck had a wide, toothed centerline belt with rough-trimmed logs on it. When the belt reached the structure Joshua stood on, it disappeared into the depths of the building, and Wolfe heard the screaming rasp of high-speed saws and smelled sawdust.

He found the second companionway and clattered down the crosshatched steel stairs.

There were three bored clerks in the office. Joshua recognized a few of the men he'd come out with in lines in front of them. He waited until one was free, then went to him and gave the man his name. The clerk touched sensors on a pad.

"You never contracted with us before," the clerk said. "Correct." It wasn't a question.

"Correct."

"Have you ever done any logging?"

"No."

"Any idea where we could plug you in?"

Joshua shrugged.

The clerk looked at a screen. "I got half a dozen slots. Four of them are in the mill here at base. Two outside. You rather work inside or out?"

"Outside."

"One's oiler on the treadway. You get bored easy?"

"Yeah."

"Then that isn't for you. You done construction?"

"Some."

"Ever drive a crane?"

"Once. Four . . . five years ago. For six months."

"You kill anybody?"

"Nobody worth mentioning."

"Pat your head and rub your gut, mister. I'm not joking."

Joshua blinked, grinned, obeyed.

"Okay," the clerk said. "You got separation there. Maybe you'll work out. One of the drivers is going below next rotation, so we need a replacement. They'll show you what you need to know up at the head. If you don't work out, report back here and we'll reassign you. That's assuming you aren't dumped for cause, in which case you go below and become their headache. Here."

He handed Joshua a blue metal disk and a red bar. He said in a bored litany: "The red one's your debit card. Buy what you want—we got a thorough company store. It'll come out of your wages before you leave or take any rotation leave below. If you lose it, you'll be responsible for any purchases made by whoever found it until you report it. The blue disk has your bunk and mess hall assignment on it. You'll sleep—" The clerk looked at his screen. "—three legs back from the head. There'll be a set of company regs on the shelf above your headboard."

"Thanks." Joshua picked up his bags.

"One other thing, Hunt. You ambitious?"

"In what way?"

"You said you like being outside. You got any interest in being a lumberpig?"

"I don't even know what he is."

"The cutter. The man down on the ground in the suit. The guy who lasers the trees that you're going to be lifting up to the Centipede."

Joshua shook his head. "Not me. Looks like a good way to get dead."

"It is. That's why we keep looking for new blood." The clerk smiled. "Sorry. Bad choice of words."

There were two smaller beltways on either side of the lumber drag. Joshua stepped on the one churning toward the end of the "Centipede" and set his bags down.

The smell of cut wood grew stronger and the clang of machinery louder as he rode.

He looked over the railing, down at the treetops. He spotted movement and saw a great leather-winged reptile with a drill-like beak hanging from a branch. Wolfe heard crashing in the jungle and looked away but could see nothing. But the tops of the trees waved frantically. He wondered what beast was passing under the shelter of the canopy.

Sitka GMBH practices the most ecologically sound lumbering possible. The use of the MaCallum-Chambers Logtrain enables you, our most important employee, to work in a relatively safe environment.

The Logtrain, sometimes humorously called the "Centipede," is built, segment by segment, from an area accessible to transports, either sea- or air-based, deep into uncut forest. It is therefore possible, from overhead, for your foremen to choose exactly the desired trees and communicate their instructions to the men on the ground, the cutters.

Once the log has been cut, it is secured by cranes at the cutting head of the Logtrain, lifted to the conveyor belt, and passed to the rear for processing.

After an area has been logged of all lumber of the type contracted for, an additional segment will be added to extend the Logtrain by you and your comrades, and once again logging will commence.

We welcome you to this, the most exciting and productive form of logging the fertile Human Mind has yet produced.

It is entirely due to the foresight and genius of Sitka GMBH Founder Harold . . .

Wolfe tossed the pamphlet aside, opened the leather-bound case, and took out a battered volume.

". . . I thought it was a place
Where life was substantial and simplified—
But the simplification took place in my memory,
I think. It seems I shall get rid of nothing,
Of none of the shadows—"

"Hey! You. Cherry boy!"

Wolfe looked up.

"You want in?" The beefy man held up the game counter. He had more bills in front of him than did the other three at the small, stained table.

"No thanks," Joshua said. "I'm not lucky."

The beefy man laughed as if Wolfe had said something funny. "You're gonna learn, out here, up near the head, we all gang together. Ain't no place for solo artists. Except maybe jackin' off. Best do what's sensible and get on over here." Two of the others laughed too loudly.

Joshua grimaced, set the book down, and got up.

"That's better," the beefy man said. "Time to learn—"

Joshua booted the chair out from under him. The man sprawled, rolled to his feet, and charged forward, roaring like a bull. Joshua knelt, sweep kicked, and the man crashed to the deck. He scrabbled up and came in again, fists milling.

Joshua's left shot out in a palm-up fist. The strike hit the man in his upper chest, the blow masking the darting motion Joshua's right hand made, two fingers tapping the beefy man's forehead.

The man's arms flew wide, and he pitched backward as if he'd run into a wall.

Joshua didn't watch him land but turned to the table. None of the other three had moved, although one man's hand was slipping toward his coverall pocket. The man's hand stopped.

Joshua waited, then went back to his book:

"... that I wanted to escape;
And, at the same time, other memories,
Earlier, forgotten, begin to return ..."

One of the gamblers went to the beefy man and began slapping his face. After a time the man groaned, sat up, then vomited explosively.

Joshua turned the page.

A violet laser blast cut through the green below and sliced sideways into the tree trunk.

"Awright," the crane driver who'd introduced himself as Lesser Eagle said. "Now, I've already got my grabs on the upper part of the log. Watch close. The pig'll cut it through on both sides ... see? It's just hanging on the stub, ready for me. Now, I'm moving in a second set of grabs just above the cut. Got it. Now, there isn't any way that goddamned log is gonna go anywhere, unless I want it to."

The suited man four hundred feet below moved hastily back as black machinery moved in on the tottering tree, a move echoed in various scales and angles by the screens around the crane cab.

There were three other cranes around the head and the same number of cutting teams down on the ground.

"I'm clear," the radio bleated.

"And I've got it," Lesser Eagle said into his mike. "Okay, I'm going to want to fell the tree to the left."

"Why left?" Joshua asked.

Lesser Eagle looked puzzled. "I can't tell you that. It's just ... the right way to do it. Maybe after you've been making lifts for six months or so, you'll get it.

"Maybe not. So when you don't know, always drop it where there's the least amount of crap. Liable to foul your lift or maybe kick up a widowmaker and take out the pig."

His hands swept across the booth's controls as if he were conducting an orchestra.

Far below the tree trunk broke from the stump to the left. The cable to the upper grab went taut, then the lower one, and the tree came up, swinging to the horizontal as it lifted toward the cutting head. Lesser Eagle swung the boom and neatly set the hundred-foot-long tree into the "basket," which in turn brought the log lumber up onto the lumber drag over Joshua's head.

"How about that, my friend? A little different than heaving iron, isn't it?"

"Not much," Joshua said. "A little hotter, a little noisier."

"Hey, Prairie Flower."

Lesser Eagle keyed his throat mike. "I'm listening, McNelly."

"I've been down for two hours. Coming up."

"Man, you ain't got no stamina," the Amerind said. "You ought to be good for a double, triple shift, the way you go on about what a great pig you are. Paul the goddamned Bunyan or whoever it was."

"Stamina my left nut. You get in this stinkin' suit one time and see how many minutes it takes you to start sweatin' off the pounds. Friggin' Sitka oughta put less money in bullshit and more into air-conditioning."

"Not a chance, McNelly. I'm one of the privileged classes. Plus you could stand to lose a few ounces.

Make you sexier next time you go below. Who's replacing you?"

"Hsui-Lee. So get ready for amateur night."

Another voice came up on the com:

"Your ass sucks buttermilk, piglet. I'll spend most of my shift cleaning up your shit. I'll be lucky if I send up more'n a few hundred feet of wood. Might as well have a brush hook as a cutter."

Wolfe heard machinery grind, and cables lifted the cutter, awkward in his bulky sealed suit, out of the jungle up toward the head of the Logtrain. Another suit came down into Wolfe's view, close enough so he could almost see through the faceplate. The pinchered arms waved or, more likely, tried to make an obscene gesture, and Hsui-Lee went down for his shift on the ground.

The monster came out of the jungle fast, a gray-green blur that hit the cutter and sent him spinning, life-support and lift cables tangling.

The radio screamed something, then cut off, then:

"Emergency! We've got a man down ... and some goddamned critter's about to take him! Where's the sonofabitchin' shooter?"

There was a gabble of chatter on the circuit that Wolfe couldn't distinguish. He was the only one in the booth—Lesser Eagle had gone to help another driver reprogram his crane, telling Wolfe to keep his goddamned hands off the controls. "Let Hsui-Lee take the wood down. We'll get it on the ground. If you want to be doing something, boom over to a clear area and practice tearing saplings out or something."

Now Wolfe could make out the horror below. It stood

about thirty feet tall, on four legs, with a body jutting up from the first two. He thought of some kind of lizardlike centaur, but the beast's upper body was a dark cylinder, its head not much more than an enormous maw of dagger fangs. Four arms scrabbled at the downed cutter.

The man's laser sliced toward the creature, cutting away one arm. Wolfe heard the nightmare roar, then his hands were busy on the controls, and the boom swung slowly, far too slowly, back from where he'd been practicing.

The cutter managed to roll away behind a tree trunk, and Wolfe had his boom over the scene. He slapped the cutaway, and his lower grab dropped, smashing down on the horror, missing the sprawled cutter by two yards.

He heard the howl through the sealed glass of the booth. His hands found another bank of controls, pulled, twisted.

The jaws of the upper grab yawned, lowered, took the monstrosity around the middle, and Wolfe lifted it clear of the ground, the cable reeling it toward him.

The grab bit deeply into the beast's side, and a greenish fluid poured out.

Joshua snapped one control up; the grab's jaws snapped open, and the horror fell, tumbling, down through the treetops into the jungle.

Wolfe saw the cables for the downed cutter's suit lift him clear of the jungle. At that moment an explosive round slammed down into the area he'd dropped the beast into, and he heard the dim blast of the gunshot from the deck above.

The booth door slid open, and Lesser Eagle burst in.

"Get the hell out of there and let me—" He stopped, realizing everything was over, and saw the limp body of Hsui-Lee moving past the booth, out of sight to the deck above. Sirens were still shrilling, and the radio was still going on about shooter failure and how in the hell and such.

"Guess you did run a crane before, eh?"

"Once or twice."

"You figure you pulled the muscle yanking that man out," the medical orderly said.

"I don't know. All I know is it's giving me grief."

"Hell. I can't see anything's wrong." The man hesitated. "But maybe I better send you back to the mill. Let a real doc make sure. I'm just the local specialist in blisters, burns, and whatever genital rots you lice managed to hide when you took your physical.

"As long as you're back there, you might want to look up Hsui-Lee. I'm pretty sure he wants to give you his firstborn or something."

"Just a sprain, Hunt," the doctor said. "You wasted your time coming back here. Get on back up to the head and tell them to put you on light duty for a day or so."

"Thanks, Doctor."

"None needed. If I hadn't heard of what you did pulling that man away from that chironosaur, I'd say you were malingering like the rest of those lice outside."

Wolfe stood, left the small clinic, and went down the corridor toward a companionway. In one hand he carried a large, heavy book. He paused outside an open door and looked in at the sleeping, bandaged man he'd last seen being dragged out of the jungle. He went on toward the deck without waking him.

The two men walked past, the first telling a most elaborate story, the second listening closely. Wolfe slipped out from his hiding place and crept to the high stack of supplies on the structure's deck. He climbed onto its top and lay flat so no one could see him.

The world was dark except for the glare of the searchlights that made a finger of light along the Centipede out into the jungle and the glare of the overhead stars.

He opened the book with the cut-out midsection, took out the small bonemike and transponder, and checked his watch. It was still a few minutes short of the hour.

He turned the set on, checked its controls, and dropped the bonemike's harness over his neck.

"Am I being listened to?" he said in Al'ar.

Nothing came for a long moment, then:

"You are being listened to," the *Grayle* said.

Joshua sagged in relief. "It would've been a real pisser," he muttered, "if this buildup hadn't paid off." Then: "Give location."

"Just entering atmosphere. I have your location. Instructions?"

"As ordered, you'll land two miles from my location, offshore, homing on this signal. Return underwater until you reach a point no more than a thousand yards distant from me, unless the water is less than a hundred feet deep. In that event, go to the nearest hundred-foot depth and remain on the bottom until summoned."

"Understood."

Joshua put away the com link to his ship and slid down from the pile of supplies. He looked out seaward, thought he saw the momentary flare of a ship's drive braking, then saw nothing. He took a tiny bottle from his book.

"Now," he said. "Now we CYA."

"I should've known," Wolfe's shift boss muttered, "you were too goddamned good to be true."

"Sorry, boss. But honest, I wasn't—"

"Hunt, don't lie to me. I can smell the stink of the booze from here. What'd you do, swim in it? Where'd you get it, anyway?"

Joshua looked down at the deck.

"Forget it," the man said. "There's never been a logger who wouldn't manage to get himself trashed if he was marooned in space. Go clean up, and in your bunk. I'm not putting you on the cutting head with a hangover. You're docked the day's wages, too.

"Lesser Eagle's covered for you, so you owe him a shift." The man scowled, then turned his attention back to the data scrolling past on his screen.

Joshua left the compartment and went down to the two-man room he'd been assigned to. His bunkie was out, working. Joshua ran a basinful of water, took off his coveralls, and began rinsing out the extract of bourbon.

"All for the shore who's going ashore," the coxswain sang out.

There were about twenty men strapped into the seats

of the small submarine, and the compartment was about half-full. No one paid any attention to the disgraced shooter who sat at the rear, cased rifle across his knees, his travel cases beside him.

The coxswain touched controls, and the port slid shut. The air-conditioning went to high.

"You know," a man sitting near Joshua said, "until you suck in good air, you forget how every friggin' breath we take stinks of that goddamned jungle."

"You been with Sitka too long," Lesser Eagle said. He sat comfortably next to the three soft cases that held his gear. "This is ship air, not the real stuff."

"And what do you think you're going to be breathing down below?" the man said.

"The same stuff," the former crane operator said. "But I'm going to be so busy making whoopee, I'll never notice."

"Bet you ten credits you're broke and back topside in a month."

"I'll take the bet," Lesser Eagle said. He grinned at Wolfe. "The man isn't aware of my resolve." He leaned toward Joshua. "You gonna look me up, in my new position of great importance, next time you come below? I'll even buy the first round. Maybe try to decoy you into staying.

"You know, only about half of the contract people fill out their time. The rest get hired away, like me.

"The only reason Sitka knows I'm leaving is the Port Authority was nice enough to buy out my obligation. Otherwise, it'd be *pfft* ... and no more Injun.

"No reason you can't follow my lead. Slinging cargo nets down there's a damn sight better than breathing wood dust and shit topside. Plus you don't get called lice and worse by the whitehats below."

"I'll keep it in mind," Wolfe said. "Thanks." He looked out the port. The sub was pulling away from the dock, out of the shadow of the Centipede. Air hissed, controls clanged, and the ocean rose and covered the port. Green changed to black as the ship dove toward the sea bottom.

"Welcome to Tworn Station," the woman said. One of the lumbermen bayed like a wolf in heat. The station greeter kept her expensive smile firmly in place.

The men swarmed out the lock into the undersea city. Wolfe stayed carefully in their midst.

The sub dock was next to the liner docks, where starships could port after they'd made the underwater approach to Tworn Station, the largest of Montana Keep's five deep-sea settlements. There was a lavish terminal there, plush welcome to the Outlaw Worlds' tourists who came to play.

Outside the terminal Wolfe noted a pair of soberly dressed, mild-looking men whose eyes seemed to meet everyone's and then sweep on.

Wind, blow, soft, not moving the grass . . .

The Chitet's gaze swept across Wolfe and moved on.

* CHAPTER EIGHTEEN *

There'd never been an Earth sky as blue as the roof of the dome. The "sun" was that of a spring morning. Wolfe consulted the map of Tworn Station he'd gotten from the Centipede's rec room, oriented himself, and started down one of the winding streets. After a few moments he stopped, frowning. He looked up, checked his watch, then looked up once more.

He remembered one of the slogans of Tworn Station: "Where the Nighttime Is the Best Time." Cleverly, while keeping to Zulu time, they'd modified it slightly. "Day" would be, he estimated, about seven-eighths normal, so the "sun's" motion was slightly accelerated. The "moon's" travel at "night" would be slowed to compensate.

From nowhere a bright ball of flame roared down. Involuntarily, he flinched just as the "comet" exploded and became flaring letters across the "sky":

GIRLS

Beautiful

227

Friendly
Lonely
All Day—All Night
Visit Neptune's Landing

Wolfe shook his head and continued walking.

Tworn Station was built in a series of not quite concentric rings. The streets wound and twisted, creating the illusion of a far larger area.

Contrary to what the logger in the submarine had said, he wasn't breathing dry, sterile ship air. Instead it sang of cinnamon, musk, cumin, watermelon—spices that tanged his nostrils and appetites.

Music roared, hummed, soared around him, coming from shops, bars, apartment buildings whose doors stood open; in them men, women, and children lounged, sharp eyes calculating, smiles offering:

"Hey, lumberpig . . . how long you been down?"

"Read your fortune, handsome?"

"Get up, get down, get all around, guaranteed pure quill, no habit, no regrets . . ."

"Best lottery odds, right here. Six winners last cycle alone . . ."

"You look lost, my friend. Need a guide?"

Wolfe kept his smile neutral, his gaze unfixed.

A woman passed, smiling a promise that her charms would more than compensate for what she'd do to his credit balance.

The buildings were low, no more than three stories at the highest. Their plas was anodized a thousand cheery colors, but not, Wolfe noted, sea-green.

He paused at the entrance to a small square. Across the way was a bar with an open terrace.

Emptiness . . . void . . . all things . . . nothing . . .

The three Chitet were looking at him. One frowned, searching her memory.

Emptiness . . . nothing . . .

Wolfe felt warmth from the Lumina in its pouch hidden behind his scrotum.

One Chitet turned to the frowning woman. "Shouldn't we be hurrying? I think we're late."

The other's frown vanished, and she checked her watch. "No," she said. "We have more than a sufficiency."

"My apologies. I misestimated. It is this strange 'sky' we are under."

The three went on.

Breathe . . . breathe . . .

"I think," Wolfe said softly, "someone besides myself may have outthought Mister Javits."

He crossed the lane and went through the outside tables and into the bar.

There was one man inside, his head on a corner table, snoring loudly. The three women at the bar spotted Wolfe. The blondest and fattest got up and came toward him, chiseling a smile through her makeup.

"Afternoon, big man. Are you as dry as I am?"

"Drier," Wolfe said. "What kind of beer do you have?"

She began a long recital. Wolfe stopped her after a few brands and chose one. She went to the bar, reached over it, touched a sensor. A few seconds later the hatch on the bar opened, and a glass with a precisely correct head on it appeared.

"I'm partial to champagne," the woman said, trying to sound throaty.

"Who isn't?" Wolfe agreed. "Buy what you really like. I'll pay champagne prices."

The woman chuckled. "I drink beer, too. But it's perdition on my hips. Easy on, hard off."

Paying no attention to her wisdom, she tapped the sensor and drank thirstily when the beer emerged.

"So you're with Sitka?"

"How'd you guess?"

"There's nothin' out-system due till tomorrow, and gen'rally, this close to the port, we get 'em first thing. How long you been loggin'?"

"Three weeks."

The woman looked disappointed.

"Something wrong with that?"

"I shouldn't say . . . but the longer you been topside, bein' chased by lizards, the readier you are to do some serious carryin' on."

"And the more credits you have to do it with," Wolfe suggested.

"That, too, honey. That, too."

Wolfe took a drink of beer.

"Who were those three prune faces that came past?" he asked. "Hard to believe they're in a place with Tworn Station's reputation."

"Hell if I know. They call themselves Chitet. Some kinda straitlaced bunch from back toward the Federation. Dunno if they're a religion or what. There's a whole cluster of 'em down here. Along with their leader.

"I read somethin' on the vid says they're here

investigatin' the possibility of settin' up their own dome. More gold to 'em, but I can't see what they'd spend their time doin' down on sea bottom.

" 'Sides poundin' their pud. They surely ain't the sort interested in ballin' the jack, man or woman. I could have more fun with a vibrator.

"Damn dull. How many of you come from topside?"

"No more'n twenty," Wolfe said.

"Damn." The woman made it into a two-syllable word. "That ain't enough for a circle jerk, let alone any kinda party. Hope to hell the liner's got some hard-chargin' folks aboard.

"So what's your pleasure, mister?" She smiled hopefully. Her breath wasn't the freshest.

"Another beer . . . and could I use your vid? I haven't been paying much attention to the world lately."

The woman looked disappointed. "Should've guessed something like that."

She brightened a little when Wolfe handed her a bill. She got him another beer and the slender plas block he'd asked for. He found a corner booth where he could see the door, sat down, and keyed the vid.

The man's expression was calm, assured. He was bald, looked to be in his early fifties, and appeared to be no more than a successful businessman. Wolfe looked more closely at the thumbnail on the vid. There must have been some glare from the camera, he decided, that created the strange glitter in the man's eyes.

He touched the sensor for PRINT instead of SPEECH, then the tellmemore.

Chitet Master Speaker Matteos Athelstan, in an exclusive interview with the *Monitor*, said he was most impressed with the citizens of Tworn Station and was so delighted with the cleanliness and recreational opportunities available under our fair dome, he said he was allowing his entire detachment, from all three of the Chitet ships currently docked at Tworn Station, liberty.

He said he hoped the citizens of Tworn Station would take the opportunity to share their lives with his men and women and expressed hope that some of our people might be interested in the Chitet philosophy, particularly as it pertained to economics.

"Very quietly, we are practicing the way of the future, leading the way out of the ruins of the past," Master Athelstan said. "Our way has already been embraced by many billions of people throughout this galaxy, and their changed lives have increased their liberty, clarity of thought, and, most importantly, economic well-being. Since my election three years ago, we've been able to increase our membership a thousandfold. In addition . . .

Wolfe touched a sensor, and the screen cleared. He keyed CALENDAR:

New Show-All Spectacular at Rodman's . . . Two-Way Theater Opens in Surround-Dome . . . Men-Only Revue and Dancing at Scandals . . . Holo-Poker at Newtons . . . Art Museum Hosts Sec-

ond Mayan Empire Display . . . The Secrets of the
Al'ar . . .

He hit PAUSE and reread the last entry carefully. He
thought for a time, trying to decide if the trap was for
him or for larger game.

Leaving his beer half-finished, he put the vid down,
got up, and left the bar.

The heavy blonde watched him leave, a sad expression
on her face. The man in the corner was still snoring.

Wolfe counted four Chitet around the main entrance
to the prefab building that had been erected on the tarmac next to the ship and guessed there'd be more.

Breathe . . . breathe . . .

His soul divided.

*Fire . . . burn low . . . burn quiet . . . embers only . . .
ready to flare . . .*

. . .

*Nothingness . . . void . . . less than space . . . all mat-
ter is here . . . there is nothing . . . no particles, no
sensation . . . the soul is vacant . . .*

A knot of tourists came down the wide avenue leading to the docks, saw the color-flashing holobanner, and
crossed to the entrance booth. Wolfe was unobtrusively
among them.

He fed coins into the slot and entered.

An Al'ar in combat harness appeared in the darkness.
Its mouth gaped and it spoke, but the words were not
the real speech but instead a simulated garble. The pur-
ported translation hissed into Wolfe's ears:

"You of the Federation . . . you have spent too long in your lazy ways . . . now we of the Al'ar have come to challenge you, to destroy you."

Wolfe's expression was blank.

"Little is known of the Al'ar ways or their culture. Only a few men and women learned their language, and even fewer were permitted to visit their worlds.

"Of those few, most were diplomats or traders, and unfortunately all too many of them were caught up and went to their deaths in the first days of the war."

Figures ran across the screen. Wolfe lifted his hand until it was silhouetted. It was trembling slightly. He watched it as if it belonged to someone else.

"After the first surprise attack," the narrator said calmly, as if the spinning, shredded Federation ships in the middle of the darkness did not exist, "and the total loss of four Federation battle fleets, humanity was put on notice that there could be but one victor and one loser in this war.

"So man girded his loins for the greatest battle that would ever be fought . . ."

There was a field of bodies.

"The Al'ar did not realize, or did not care, that these men and women were trying to surrender.

"But there was a worse fate than death. Some humans were captured by the Al'ar. No one knows what tortures they were subjected to, for only a few were rescued or managed to escape."

The screen showed a slumped woman. Involuntarily,

Joshua flinched. Twelve years before he had led the team that had rescued her and three others.

Breathe ... breathe ...

The red blotches on the starchart shrank and shrank.

"Little by little," the narrator went on, "we drove them back and back, off the worlds they'd conquered, back from their outpost planets, and we attacked what the Al'ar called their capital worlds.

"The Federation came in for the death stroke. Huge fleets, thousands of ships, many millions of fighting men and women closed in for the final assault on the Al'ar sanctuaries.

"And then ... then the Al'ar disappeared.

"No one knows where they went. The ships offworld exploded as one, as if they'd all had bombs aboard, fused to detonate at the same time.

"The handful of Al'ar we'd managed to capture simply disappeared. No prison camp sensor showed any sign of where they could have gone.

"Similarly, when reconnaissance teams were sent down onto the Al'ar capital worlds, they found nothing.

"There are tales that food was found on tables, that Al'ar machinery was running, that their weather control apparatus was in operation.

"These are all false. In fact, it was as if the Al'ar had decided to leave and, before their departure, had cleaned, shut everything down ... and then simply vanished.

"Where did they go?

"Why did they go?

"There are no answers.

"The Al'ar are gone ... and they took their secrets with them."

The starchart vanished. There was blackness, then the lights came up. There were only a handful of people in the circular theater with Wolfe. One of them was a Chitet who looked at Wolfe but did not see him.

"You are invited to visit our museum behind this chamber," the synthed voice said. "Also, on your way out, we welcome you to our gift shop and hope you will recommend our exhibition to your friends."

"Not bloody likely," one of the tourists who'd entered in front of Joshua grumbled. "Secrets of the Al'ar ... by Mohamet, I thought we'd find out how they screwed or something.

"This is just like friggin' school and history shit!"

His friends laughed, agreed, and went out.

Joshua lingered in the narrow corridors of what the voice had called a museum, paying little attention to the mostly false relics, the battle souvenirs, the holopics, which were as tacky as everything else in the show.

He *felt* something—he didn't know what.

Not fire ... not water ... not void ... not earth ... not air ...

His hands were curled, held slightly away from his body. He walked strangely, each foot sweeping in, almost touching the other, then out into a wide-legged stance.

There was something ...

There was nothing ...

He came to a passage, looked down it, took a step.

A wall fell away, and the Al'ar came at him, its grasping organ blurred in a death strike.

* CHAPTER NINETEEN *

But Wolfe wasn't there to accept the strike.

He ducked, stepped in, and stood, launching his own attack. But the Al'ar had stopped in midstrike and spun away.

Time found a stop.

Wolfe was the first to speak.

"Taen!"

The Al'ar's head moved slightly. His hood was fully flared.

"You have 'seen' me, Shadow Warrior." The Al'ar changed to Terran. **"And I recognize you, Joshua Wolfe."**

Neither relaxed.

"Have you come to kill me?"

"I was hired for that task . . . not knowing it was you I would find. But it is not a duty my body shall fulfill."

The Al'ar slightly lowered his grasping organs. "I

237

should have known that if you survived the war, you would be the one to find me."

"How did you live?" Wolfe asked.

"Better to ask why," Taen said. "Although that is a question I do not know the answer to. Please speak Terran. For the moment I do not wish to be reminded of what is in the past."

"Sentiment? From an Al'ar?"

"Perhaps. Perhaps that is why I was . . . left," Taen said. "Perhaps I had become tainted by my interest in the life of groundworms. Perhaps I was deemed unworthy to make the Crossing. Or perhaps there is another meaning I have not yet discovered."

"You know you're in one hell of a trap," Wolfe said. "And now I'm in it with you."

"Those men who dress like **hanthglaw**?"

"Yes. They call themselves Chitet." Wolfe half smiled, remembering the Al'ar primitive creature who kept the colors of whatever he slid across.

"I first *felt* someone was on my trail some time ago," Taen said. "When I *felt* you enter my realm, my exhibition, I thought you were the only hunter. But now I can *feel* the others out there.

"It is truly an excellent trap, well laid to take us both, here beneath the water, inside this dome. I fear we shall have to abandon this craft. Not that it matters. I have Federation monies to build a hundred more like it and know the location of many derelicts.

"But that is for the future, and their plan will not be set in motion for a time, so we may speak of the past and determine what actions must be taken next.

"It will take some cleverness for us to escape this

snare of theirs. Unless you wish to reverse your intent and attempt to continue the task you were first set and grant me the death. I will warn you, I do not think you can accomplish it, even though your movements are far better than when last we exchanged blows in learning."

"I do not intend to kill you. And the Chitet weren't the ones who hired me."

"The Federation?"

"Yes."

"So where do these Chitet come into consideration?"

"I don't know exactly. They captured me on a world called Trinité and interrogated me."

"So it was you who caused all the upset with exploding spaceships and such matters. I saw some of what had happened on the vid and decided that that was no place for one such as myself to appear, even though I thought it had great promise in my search.

"So like a gowk, instead of—what is your phrase?—going to ground and seeing what would come next, I continued my rounds.

"You see how blind a being can become when he is alone and frantic?"

"I never heard you talk like this."

"I was never unable to *feel* another one like myself, either."

"You said the Crossing. What does that mean?"

"Those are the . . . realms, but that is not the correct word, and I find none in my Terran speech . . . for where my people have gone. But they have gone on, as they once entered your space."

Wolfe stared at the Al'ar for a long time. "You—your people—were not of this spacetime?"

"Of course not. How else were we able to move on so easily? Although this time it was into a far different dimension than what you term spacetime."

"Are they gone for good?"

"Yes. Or, I think so. Let me give you a comparison that you showed me once in one of your books of Earth. Can a butterfly become a larva? Even though what happened cannot be compared to a growing. It was merely a necessary change."

"Because we were about to defeat you?"

Taen was silent for a long time. He moved his grasping organs together, rustling, like dry wheat.

"Just so. Just as we were forced out of our previous . . . dimension."

"This is a great deal to understand," Joshua said. "And I think I now know more than any other man."

"That is not unlikely. So come. I will make you a vessel of that potion you so loathed and forced yourself to drink to learn more about us."

Joshua managed a smile. "At least, drinking that **valta** crap, I won't know if you've poisoned me."

"That thought occurred to me as well."

"It is as terrible as I remember it," Wolfe said, sipping. "Worse, even."

"I often wish," Taen said, "I could have understood what you termed humor. It seemed a comfort in times of great stress to your people, and I thought it might be helpful to me.

"But there is no such possibility."

The two had left the museum and gone back through the building that extended from and was part of Taen's ship. It was the same one Wolfe had seen in Cisco's projection, a time that now seemed far distant.

The Federation craft had been modified internally until it had duplicated Al'ar ships Wolfe had been aboard, bare except for controls and minimal comforts, walls moving with ever-changing eye-disturbing colors. Taen crouched on the spidery rack the Al'ar used to relax on. Wolfe perched on another unit.

"When the war began," Taen said without preamble, "I was considered suspect. Perhaps it was because I attempted to speak to the Elders about you and your family and others. They thought I had become contaminated.

"I had not. I merely knew if we did not treat nonfighters with what you told me was called kindness, the Federation forces would fight more strongly, more cleverly.

"But they paid no mind, and so the situation was as I predicted."

"You know my parents died in the camp."

Taen inclined his head but made no response for a moment. "I did not know that. But I knew that you escaped. That was when they allowed me to become a fighter, after the Elders had seen evidence of your thinking, of what we had taught you. I was put in charge of a unit intended to find and destroy you."

"I wondered," Wolfe said, "about something like that. As the war went on, several of the . . . projects I mounted encountered difficulties. I thought then that possibly you, or some of your other broodmates I met and sparred with, had been tasked to hunt me."

"But we never came close," Taen said. "I think we

held you in too much contempt, as we held all Terrans. After a time the unit was broken up, and we were sent to other duties.

"I became a ... a predictor of events. When your fleets closed on Sauros, I was in a tiny ship, one that even your sensors could not detect, far offworld, waiting to give estimations of vulnerability to our fleet commanders. The link was sealed ... and then ... then I lost all contact."

Once more Taen moved his grasping organs together. Wolfe felt dryness, despair, a dying echo, across the chamber.

"Strange," he said. "I was just below you. On the ground. Doing much the same task."

The Al'ar uncoiled violently from the rack, eye slits wide, hood flaring. "What did you see? What happened?"

Joshua thought he could *feel*, behind the toneless Al'ar accents, desperation.

"I saw nothing. I was hidden. All I knew was that all your jamming, all the communication bands I was monitoring went blank.

"Then there was nothing."

Taen returned to his perch. "Then there was nothing," he echoed.

Joshua picked up the bowl again and sipped at the sharp bitterness of the **valta**. "What did you do then?"

"I waited until my screens showed that all Federation ships had left the system. I used my emergency power to land on Sauros and find a ship.

"That ship led me to another, one of the Federation

ships we had captured and outfitted as a decoy. This craft.

"I fled deeper into our space to a factory world. I activated the machines, set them to building this . . . mummery, I think is the word. I had the machines build me other machines so all this could be run by one being, and actually I am not required beyond the instant to start the apparatus. All else is automated, roboticized. The idea came to me within a short time after my people had . . . left."

Wolfe had the queer idea that Taen had wanted to say "abandoned me." He said nothing.

"Since I must travel in the ways of the groundworms, I remembered a story you had once told me, about how a smart Terran hid something from someone right out in the open. That is why *The Secrets of the Al'ar* came to be. Who would dream an Al'ar would dare to display himself so openly?

"Perhaps the idea is clever, although I must tell you, if I shared any of the emotions you tried to tell me about, disgust would match my sentiments as to what I am doing."

"That's the question," Wolfe said. "Why are you doing what you're doing? What are you looking for?"

"I do not know if I should tell you that. But I knew the link, the place I would find a clue, would be somewhere between the worlds of the Al'ar and the worlds of man. I will find a matrix someday.

"I must."

Once more Wolfe felt desperation.

"I didn't tell you," he said, "just what the Chitet were

interested in." He stood, turned his back, unfastened his clothes, and took out the Lumina.

"Ah," Taen said. "You have one of the stones I sold for my expenses. I would guess you have been using it to increase your powers."

"How did you sell them?"

"It took me a time to establish a method. I watched those who came to see my show, then utilized the resources any computer can access to find out more about them.

"Eventually I found a man more interested in money than in where the Luminas came from or who provided them. He had no problem doing business with a being he never met, never even saw on a vid screen. He remained honest only because he knew if he cheated me, his source of riches would vanish. No doubt he also assumed that I would hunt him down and slay him.

"Unfortunately, he died in what appeared tó be an accident some time ago. I should have been suspicious and investigated more fully.

"No doubt if I had, I would have discovered the presence of these Chitet earlier."

"Taen, you are trying to avoid what we must talk about. The Chitet asked me about a Mother Lumina, something they also called the Overlord Stone."

Taen made no response.

"Another man, a man the Chitet murdered, was looking for the same thing. Is that what you want, Taen? Is that what you're looking for?"

"That is what I seek," the Al'ar said reluctantly.

"For what end?"

"I am not sure yet. But it has a . . . congruence on the Crossing."

"Will you know what to do with it when you find it?"

Taen turned his face away from Wolfe, hood inflating slightly.

"Goddamit, answer me!"

"No," the Al'ar answered. "But there will be those who shall."

"Other Al'ar?"

"Yes. Not all of us were permitted to cross."

"Who are these others?"

"I do not know them. I was never told directly of them. But they are the Guardians.

"If they exist, if what I believe is the truth and not a story that keeps me from turning on myself and tearing my own vessels of life apart."

"Other Al'ar," Wolfe said, returning to Terran. "Why did they remain? What are they guarding? Why was this Overlord Stone left behind?"

"I do not know the answers to any of your questions. When—if—I find the Mother Lumina, perhaps I shall hold some.

"But I *feel* we are running short of time. This dome's day ends. These docks will be deserted soon. Then they shall attack.

"We must ready our welcome."

* CHAPTER TWENTY *

"We may have one slight advantage," Joshua said. "Since we have information they want—or you do, anyway—they'll be trying to take us alive."

Taen held out grasping organs, moved them from side to side: scorn.

"It has been far too long since you have been subjected to the inexorable logic of war. Perhaps you no longer deserve your Al'ar name.

"I am the one with the knowledge, or so they must believe. Therefore, your presence becomes superfluous."

"Thanks for the correction," Wolfe said dryly. "Not that I planned to be around for further tender mercies in an interrogation chamber."

"Nor I, although no Terran can know how to torture an Al'ar."

"And thus we reassure the other." Wolfe once more checked the loading of the medium blaster he'd smuggled down from topside and then inserted gas plugs in each nostril.

"I have a question, Shadow Warrior. I have a special suit that I wear when I fear being seen by Terrans. It gives me a very human appearance. Should I don it? I would rather not, since it restricts my movements."

Joshua considered, then grinned. "Go naked. The shock value might keep both of us alive a few seconds longer."

"That is a cunning thought," Taen said.

The Lumina on the table flared.

"Do you have any idea what that might signify?" the Al'ar asked.

"Not sure," Wolfe said. "But I'd guess the Chitet have a Lumina of their own. Probably they're sitting around staring at it, thinking into it, hoping it's some kind of weapon. I doubt they've had a lot of one-on-one contact with Al'ar before. For all I know, they think they've got some kind of crystal ball."

"Which is?"

"Something frauds use to befuddle fools by pretending to predict the future.

"All we need to know is they're getting ready to hit us."

"Since no one knows the exact power of a Lumina," Taen said, "I'd first suggest that we communicate only in Terran, unless circumstances dictate otherwise. Perhaps they might be able to track me by my speech. I do not know. But I think it is time to take some action to disrupt their strategy.

"If the station authorities had not disabled my drive

when they permitted me to bring my ship into the station, the solution would be simple. I have more than enough power to punch through this dome."

Wolfe stared at the Al'ar. "And what about the ten thousand or so people in the dome who don't share our feud?"

"What matter they? I do not know them. And they are not Al'ar."

"Sometimes I forget," Wolfe said, "just what made your people so lovable.

"But there's an idea there."

There were three "moons" overhead: violet, orange, yellow. The programmers of Tworn Station had decided to add exotica to this "night."

The ship and its attached, extended structure sat in dimness. There were overhead lights along the lanes on either side of the square, and other lights gleamed from the nearby port terminal.

A few passersby paused, looked at the darkened marquee with disappointment, and looked for other pleasures.

Music came faintly, dissonantly, perhaps from a distant calliope.

Here and there in the shadows there was slight movement. A gun barrel gleamed, moved back into darkness.

A tiny hatch atop the ship's hull opened, was seen.

"Stand by," a Chitet section leader said into his throatmike.

Something soared out, throwing sparks, smashed into the top of the dome, and bounced back, and the signal flare exploded. White light flooded the station, brighter than the "sun's" day.

Night observation devices flared, overloaded, went to black, died. Men and women staggered, blinded, seeing nothing but red.

The ship's hatch slid open, and two beings darted out, bent low. A blaster bolt smashed into the deck beside them.

"Only the Terran," Wolfe heard someone shout. "Don't shoot unless you're sure!"

A man came up, pistol in a two-handed grip, and Wolfe cut him down. There was a woman behind him, aiming a gas projector. She fired, and the projectile bounced out, spraying a white fog. Taen's weapon, a long slender tube that fitted over one of his grasping organs, buzzed, and the woman screamed and fell, most of her chest seared off.

They ran down the passage, hearing shouts and the clattering boot heels of pursuit.

"You should have walked your escape route as I did," Taen said.

"I . . . wasn't planning on getting out this way," Wolfe panted. He turned, sent four bolts at random to the rear, and ran on.

There were milling men and women coming out of doorways, shouting, screaming as the flare overhead died. Some recognized the corpse-white Al'ar, and their shrieks added a new terror to the swirling throng. Gunfire boomed, the screams grew louder, and Wolfe saw a young man gape in disbelief at the bloody mess that had been his knee.

They came to an open square with a deserted bandstand in its center. They ran toward the bandstand, and six Chitet rose from concealment and rushed forward, encircling them.

Wolfe went airborne, his feet lashed out, and he felt bones shatter. He let himself land on the body, scissor kicked the second attacker's feet out, and pulled the woman down on him as the third's rifle butt crashed down.

The woman grunted, and Joshua rolled from under her and was up. He sidestepped the weapon's butt strike. His hand reached and then touched the rifleman's elbow; he shouted, and the weapon fell from pain-numbed fingers.

Wolfe's right hand came out in a finger strike, and the man bent double, trying to suck in the air denied him as Wolfe's left hand tapped the back of his skull; the corpse fell limply to the decking.

Wolfe recovered and saw the fifth man's body spasm as if electrocuted. Taen's grasping organ flashed out once more, and the sixth Chitet contorted and dropped.

Wolfe and Taen ducked for cover, and a blaster bolt from behind crashed into the plas wall above them.

"We appear to be cut off," Taen said, and fired a long burst behind himself.

Not far from the blackened crater the bolt had made was a panel, one of hundreds scattered through Tworn Station. Wolfe had seen them; then their commonality had made them invisible.

On the panel were three sealed boxes, one labeled FIRE, the second DOME LEAK, the third GAS. Under them was a warning:

EMERGENCY ONLY
Any person who knowingly sets
off a false alarm will be prosecuted
to the fullest extent of the
Tworn Station Authority.
The most severe penalties will be sought,
including fines, imprisonment, loss of citizenship,
and banishment for life.

"When in doubt," Wolfe murmured, and shot all three boxes open.

The night went mad. Sirens howled, screamed, clanged. Doors crashed shut. Partitions arched up from the deck, closing off the dome.

"Come on! For the port!"

Lasers flashed overhead, to the side, and then steel walls rose smoothly, above a man's height, blocking Chitet pursuit, continued to rise higher still until they touched the "sky," partitioning the dome and sealing Tworn Station against the anticipated blowout.

Wolfe ran for the dome wall, pushing his way through the crowd that had poured from nowhere.

"To your stations! Emergency stations!" a man bayed. He saw Wolfe, the gun, then the Al'ar. He screamed something, reached into a pocket, and Wolfe snap kicked him into a wall.

The dome wall was just ahead, and a blister yawned open.

"Inside!"

They dove into the survival pod as a gun blasted behind them. The pod was a thirty-foot-long cylinder with a rounded front and a squared rear. There were four rows of plas seats with safety harness and a small control panel with a single porthole above it. The air lock's gray metal was visible outside. Wolfe slammed the SEAL sensor, and the pod's hatch hissed closed.

"Did you know this was here?" Taen asked.

"I didn't. But there had to be something," Joshua said. "Shut up. I'm trying to figure out how this bastard works."

He scanned the panel, ignoring the flashing lights, touched sensors, swore when nothing happened.

One panel was blinking insistently:

DO NOT LAUNCH WITHOUT AUTHORITY PERMISSION!
DO NOT LAUNCH WITHOUT AUTHORITY PERMISSION!

There was a crash as the unknown gunman outside sent another shot into the pod.

"Over there?" Taen suggested.

Under the controls was a square box marked OVER-RIDE. Wolfe ripped it open, saw old-fashioned manual knife switches, and snapped them closed.

The world lurched beneath him as the pod rolled out into the lock. Wolfe heard the clunks of another pod being moved into position as the lock cycled them out of the dome. Water frothed outside, rising to cover the porthole, and there was nothing but black.

Again the world roiled, and he stumbled, grabbing one of the plas seats to steady himself.

Taen curled himself into one of the seats.

"Your departure from the station was successful," a synthed voice intoned. "Alarm signals on all standard distress frequencies are being automatically broadcast."

Wolfe swallowed, equalizing pressure as the pod shot toward the surface.

"And what happens next?"

"We surface, and I call for my ship. Then we get the hell out of Dodge."

"And after that? What are your long-range plans?"

"I would dearly like," Wolfe said, "to see tomorrow or maybe the week afterward." He became serious. "I don't *have* many options. Federation Intelligence will be after me for not killing you, and the Chitet won't give up.

"I guess there's only two things possible: Either I start practicing how to become invisible on a full-time basis or else go looking for this goddamned Mother Lumina that's got everyone on a skewed orbit."

"Are you suggesting," Taen said, "that you become my partner in my quest?"

"If you wish me to," Joshua said carefully. The subject seemed better handled in his second tongue.

"At one time, when we were little more than hatchlings," Taen said, "I wondered what a partnership would have produced, when we achieved full growth. But I thought in terms of exploration of the unknown or something of that nature, and when I realized we were doomed to go to war with each other . . ."

Joshua waited, but the Al'ar did not finish the sentence. After a heavy silence, Taen continued:

"But I have allowed the dead past to swallow me.

"I observed the way you fought down below. You are a far greater warrior than when last I saw you. You have learned much with no one to guide you. You give great honor to your teachers, your fellow students who tried to help you learn the ways of fighting.

"To answer your question, yes, of course. I welcome you, Shadow Warrior, and it is my honor to be allowed to fight with you."

Something touched Wolfe, something he had not felt for time beyond memory.

"We are approaching the ocean's surface," the artificial voice said. "Would all aboard strap themselves down, in the event of bad weather on the surface, to avoid injury. One person designated as pod control officer should approach the controls."

A board slid out from the control panel.

"This pod has a range of approximately a hundred miles at a fixed speed of three knots. You will observe the controls provided."

There was a joystick, a dial with a pointer, and a single slidepot.

"The stick functions as a rudder, and the other control is a throttle. Use these to steer your craft.

"Warning—do not expend your fuel foolishly. If there is a storm, do not attempt to sail out of it but wait until it has passed.

"The third instrument indicates the nearest broadcast point. Keep the red arrow centered at the top of the dial and you will go toward it.

"It is not likely that you will reach that point, however, since all stations on Montana Keep have been alerted to the emergency.

"Do not become alarmed. You will be rescued in short order." The program shut down.

"Wonderful," Wolfe said. "As if we need to advertise."

He looked for anything that might access the pod's transmitter, saw nothing.

"We have worse problems," Taen said. "Look at the hatchway."

Wolfe turned and saw water seeping into the pod.

He hurried to the hatch. Halfway down it the metal was torn, blackened. Along the edge was torn, burned sealant with water beading through.

"Our friend was a better shot than I thought," he said. Suddenly the metal wrenched farther open, and a stream of water gushed in, sending him staggering back.

"Can we block this?" he shouted over the building hiss of the incoming ocean.

"I see nothing," Taen said.

The pod chamber was rapidly filling, water almost knee-deep now. Wolfe sloshed to the control panel, stared out and up. The blackness was less absolute, and he thought he saw light above. He felt pain in his chest, realized the pod's atmospheric equalizer must've been hit as well, and began exhaling steadily.

"Breathe . . . out . . ." he managed. "Or . . . rupture whatever . . . kind of lungs . . . you've got . . ."

"The question would appear to be," Taen said, undisturbed, **"whether we gather enough water to keep us from rising before or after we reach the surface."**

The blackness *was* lighter, and then daylight blinded them. The pod shot clear of the water, then crashed back down. Wolfe was slammed into a wall, and his vision darkened, then came back. He looked out the porthole. The ocean was gray, with a small chop.

"Are we still leaking?"

Taen waded to the hatch. "How interesting," he said. "I can observe the ocean beyond. It would appear that the hole is just above the water level, although waves are bringing in water every now and again. If we had pumps, we could pump it dry and be safe."

"That's one of the many things we're a bit short of," Wolfe said. The control panel's directional needle was pointing to the right. He slid the control pot up to full, turned the joystick, and centered the needle.

He heard humming, and slowly, laboriously, the pod began moving, the water level now just below the smashed hatch.

You are in the sea . . . so you have allowed it to embrace you . . . turn away . . . you are letting it wash you, move you . . . you are not in control now . . . you are not part of the tide . . . reach for the earth, remember the earth, find your center . . . find the void . . . return whole . . .

His breathing slowed. He *felt* out, found nothing. He took the Lumina from his pocket, held it, not seeing it flame up.

Taen said something, and Wolfe *felt* surprise in his words but did not allow them to be heard.

Beyond there . . . out there . . . land . . . the jungle . . . the earth . . . feel on . . .

Involuntarily Wolfe swiveled, *felt* where the Centipede lay on the continent that stretched in front of him, *felt* its distance.

"As a good guess," he said, "we're only about ten, twelve miles from the lumber station where I came down to Tworn Station." He touched the plas that concealed the bonemike and winced as his fingers found a deep gouge in its surface that had been cut without his realizing it.

"Ship, do you hear me?"

There was no response.

"Ship, do you understand this sending?"

Again, nothing.

"Ship, can you detect this device singing to you? Respond at once on this frequency."

"I hear a singing in a tongue none speak," came the response. *"I am responding only because my logical circuits dictate you must be the one sending. If that was you sending previously, be advised your voice pattern no longer matches the one I am required to obey. Please inform problem. Be advised if input does not give satisfactory explanation, all transmissions from your station will be ignored."*

"The transponder suffered physical damage. Do not terminate transmission. That is an order. Emergency override," and Wolfe switched to Terran, "Frangible, Onyx, Three, Phlebas."

"Your message received, understood. Emergency override orders acknowledged. Stress analysis applied. No sign evident that you are drugged or under control of a hostile. As instructed, I will obey your orders."

"Shit," Joshua muttered. "I think I'm a little too careful. Ship, do you have this station located?"

"I do."

"Lift from the bottom but do not break surface until you're a mile offshore. Then, at full power—"

Static suddenly roared against his bones.

"Ship, do you receive this station?"

He felt nothing but the static.

"What is it?"

"I'm not sure," Wolfe said. "I hope it's just some kind of local interference. But I'll bet I'm wrong. We've got troubles, partner. I think somebody picked up our transmission and is jamming it."

"The Chitet?"

Wolfe shrugged. "I guess our best chance is to ride this clunker to shore, hope the jamming stops, then call again."

Taen's hood lifted, subsided.

"Then that is what we shall do."

Thirty minutes later Wolfe saw the outline of the coast rise out of the gray water ahead. He couldn't make out the Centipede yet but kept the needle centered. Less than five minutes after that the steady hum of the drive faltered, then quit. The pod settled, and water began slopping through the hatch.

"We took a harder hit than I thought," he said. "How are you at swimming?"

"I will float under this planet's circumstances," the Al'ar said. "However, propelling myself through the water will be a very slow matter." He held out his slender grasping organs. "But I shall kick and flail as best I can."

"The hell you will," Wolfe said. "I'll tow you. Let's get this hatch open and out of here."

He hit the sensor. Motors hummed, and the hatch moved, opening a few inches; then metal grated against metal. He hit the sensor again and heard a relay cut out.

"We may not have to worry about swimming," he

muttered. He braced against one of the plas seats, kicked, kicked again. The inner surface of the hatch caved in a bit but didn't open.

Taen stepped in front of him and slid his impossibly slender grasping organs through the slit. He braced himself against one wall and pulled.

Joshua felt the Lumina in his pocket flame, heat. Metal screeched, and the hatch moved a few inches; then the relay cut back in, and the way was open and the ocean crashed in. The pod rolled, began sinking.

Joshua had an arm around the Al'ar's thin chest. He pushed his way out, against the current, and was out of the survival pod.

He fought his way to the surface, swam a few strokes away from the sinking pod, and released Taen. He rolled on his back, forced his boots off, and let them sink. He unbuckled his gun belt, was about to release it, and stopped. He looped the belt around his neck and buckled it.

"Now we swim?" Taen inquired.

There was still nothing but the jamming roar to be felt through the transponder.

"Now we swim. You lie on your back, keep your head above water, and kick with me. Sooner or later we'll either drown or hit the beach."

"I shall not drown."

Wolfe wondered what Taen meant, then put the matter out of mind.

Reach deep ... the way is long ... you have much power ... your muscles are not torn, not aching ... this is sport ... breathe ... breathe ... now feel the sea, let it take you, let it wash you ...

The pod was barely visible above the surface, rolling, about to sink, no more than thirty feet away.

A gray-green snake's head as big as Wolfe's body broke the surface, reaching ten feet into the air on a snake neck. Wolfe saw a flipper break the surface and turn the creature.

It glared down at the pod, hissed a challenge, struck, and screeched its agony as teeth chipped against the alloy steel. It struck once more, then turned, seeing the two beings in the water.

Wolfe's fingers fumbled for the holster catch, lifting the retaining loop. The sea monster's head lashed down; its fanged mouth struck the water just short of Taen. The Al'ar slapped the beast on the top of its jaws, a seeming touch.

Wolfe heard bones crunch, and the creature screamed and rolled over, showing a light green belly and four thrashing flippers. It came back up, shrilling, and pulled its head back like a cobra about to lunge.

Wolfe had his pistol out and touched the stud. A wave washed his arm, and the blast slammed past the monster's neck. He fired once more, and the bolt hit the animal just below its skull. Ichor gouted over the water around them, and the animal thrashed, slamming into the sinking pod again and again.

Wolfe had Taen around the neck and was swimming hard, away from the pooling gore and the sea monster's death throes.

"I don't," he managed, "want to see what this world imagines sharks to be like."

"Do not speak," Taen said. "Reserve your strength for the task ahead."

Wolfe obeyed and let his free arm and legs move, move in muscle memory.

He fancied he could see the tree line ahead of him but knew better, for they were still too far out. He refused to allow himself hope, reminded his mind it was a drunken, careening monkey, swam on.

It might have been five strokes, it might have been five thousand, when the sky darkened.

Wolfe rolled on his back and saw the great ship descending toward them.

"Are we being rescued?"

Wolfe brought his mind back from where he had buried it and studied the starship through salt-burning eyes.

"No," he said. "That's an old Federation cruiser. *Ashida* class, I'm pretty sure."

"Then release me. I shall go down to my death before I go into the hands of the Federation."

"You don't have to worry about that," Wolfe said. "All of them got mothballed or broken up for scrap after the war. But this one didn't."

"Chitet!"

The static blur against his clavicle was gone, and a voice sounded:

"Stand by for pickup. If you have weapons, discard them. Any attempts at resistance will only produce your deaths. I say again, stand by for pickup."

Wolfe had the pistol out, held just below the water.

"No," Taen said. "Release the weapon. They will only shoot us in the water. Is it not better to let them pick us up and then meet our deaths when we have a better chance of taking some of them along to amuse us on our journey?"

Wolfe opened his fingers, saw the pistol sink down into green darkness.

The huge ship was only fifty feet above them, moving to one side, when the *Grayle* broke water, its hatch sliding open, less than ten feet away.

Wolfe was swimming desperately, once more grasping Taen as he felt heat from the Chitet cruiser's drive sear him. He found a grab rail, pulled himself aboard, and rolled into the lock.

It cycled close behind him.

"Lift," he gasped. "Straight off the water, full evasive pattern."

"Understood."

Gravity twisted and warped; then the ship's AG took over, and he came to his feet.

"Screens!" He saw the bulk of the ship nearly overhead, to one side, the land, the sea below. The *Grayle* was skimming just above the water, accelerating.

Water spouted high to the right, where the *Grayle* would have been if it hadn't jinked a second earlier. On another screen he saw the cruiser's missile port snap closed and another open.

"Immelman, straight back at them."

"Understood."

He felt vertigo even through the artificial gravity as the ship climbed and rolled.

He grabbed a railing for support. Taen crouched on the deck nearby.

"Target . . . starship ahead."

"Acquired."

"Launch one!"

The cruiser was no more than ten miles distant when one of the *Grayle*'s tubes spat fire and the air-to-air missile smashed toward it.

Whoever was controlling the ship was very fast, recovering from amazement at receiving fire from what appeared to be no more than a yacht, and the former Federation warship banked away, climbing.

But Wolfe's missile couldn't miss at that range. It exploded into the Chitet cruiser near the stern, and the ship twisted in the blast.

"Offplanet!"

"Understood."

The *Grayle* climbed at full drive.

In a side and then a rear screen, Joshua watched the Chitet ship flounder like a gaffed fish, smoke pouring from its wound.

The ship grew smaller, smaller still, and then they were in space.

"Three jumps. At random. No destination."

"Understood."

Joshua looked at Taen as the Al'ar got to his feet. He was suddenly very tired.

He *felt* Taen's strength and a chilly, almost robotic companionship.

"And now it begins," the Al'ar said.

"Now it begins," Joshua echoed.

The *Grayle* vanished into the cold fire of the stars.

About the Author

CHRIS BUNCH lives in a tiny village on the Washington coast and collects artillery and enemies. This is his seventeenth book.

DEL REY ONLINE!

The Del Rey Internet Newsletter...

A monthly electronic publication, posted on the Internet, GEnie, CompuServe, BIX, various BBSs, and the Panix gopher (gopher.panix.com). It features hype-free descriptions of books that are new in the stores, a list of our upcoming books, special announcements, a signing/reading/convention-attendance schedule for Del Rey authors, "In Depth" essays in which professionals in the field (authors, artists, designers, sales people, etc.) talk about their jobs in science fiction, a question-and-answer section, behind-the-scenes looks at sf publishing, and more!

Online editorial presence: Many of the Del Rey editors are online, on the Internet, GEnie, CompuServe, America Online, and Delphi. There is a Del Rey topic on GEnie and a Del Rey folder on America Online.

Our official e-mail address for Del Rey Books is delrey@randomhouse.com

Internet information source!

A lot of Del Rey material is available to the Internet on a gopher server: all back issues and the current issue of the Del Rey Internet Newsletter, a description of the DRIN and summaries of all the issues' contents, sample chapters of upcoming or current books (readable or downloadable for free), submission requirements, mail-order information, and much more. We will be adding more items of all sorts (mostly new DRINs and sample chapters) regularly. The address of the gopher is **gopher.panix.com**

Why? We at Del Rey realize that the networks are the medium of the future. That's where you'll find us promoting our books, socializing with others in the sf field, and—most importantly—making contact and sharing information with sf readers.

For more information, e-mail ekh@panix.com